Eltopia

Works by E. Hank Buchmann

Darling Liberty
Until the Names Grow Blurred
The Homing
Nightly Crossings
Lila B.
A River Death
Following Capella
Love & War
Empire
Natives of Lost Places
Benchmarks

Marshal Boone Crowe western series
writing as Buck Edwards

Dead Woman Creek
Showdown in the Bear Grass
Judgment at Rattlesnake Wash
Track of the Wolf
The Widow Makers
Shootout at Lost River
5 Bullets

Eltopia

E. Hank Buchmann

As fathers go, I had the best.
This book is dedicated to the memory of Edward H. Buchmann,
a man who knew and loved this high desert country
and the garden oasis it became.

The sound of rain wakes me, it's abrupt, growing pulse against the shutters, against the panes. And I am sometimes confused at that early hour. Waking, I think perhaps I am hearing the rain of Eltopia, dashing its summer vengeance through the trees, thrashing against the clapboards and windows of that dark house, on that long-ago dark night. Or is it the soft, deadly fall of snow on Bastogne, falling on my father in his foxhole, 1944? Could it be falling on me in my bed, through some dim time-tunnel, unwrapping me slowly from my sleeping grief, connecting me to his absence once more?

When this happens, I leave my bed, and wrapping my robe around me I trudge down the hall to my study and wait for the first glimpse of dawn through my east window. My wife knows how this works with me, so she rarely stirs, knowing, even in her sleep, that I need this time alone. From our hill on Francis Street, I can get a fair view of the Ohio River in the distance, and the lights of greater Cincinnati reflecting off it. If one does not read the newspapers or watch the evening news, Cincinnati can be a beautiful city. And that is how I prefer to love her, apart from her sometimes sad affairs. It is her history I love. And that is why I teach it—Cincinnati's history, and the great country that she is a part of.

My classroom at Whittier High School is on the second floor and overlooks the baseball practice grounds and the field house. In the spring, after last bell, I enjoy standing at that window, watching the green freshmen running drills, their hearts big with hope. They might have been my boys, if I was still thirty, or forty, still coaching, whistle around my neck, using a dinged-up bat as a pointer, directing traffic. But yesterday my classroom door opened, disturbing this sweet reverie. Olive Nettles, an after-school office runner, and one of my brighter senior girls from second period, approached me, apologetically, with outstretched arm. In her hand was a piece of paper, and waving it gently, seemed eager to be rid of it.

"What have we here, Olive?" I asked, teasing her into prolonging her shyness.

"I don't know, Mr. Witt. Mrs. Stewart just said for me to bring it."

"And you have. Thank you, Olive."

Alone again I took my first long look at it, and thought for a minute it might be a joke. In the age of technology; of email and cell phones, and everything else, I found I was holding a Western Union telegram. Did people even send telegrams anymore? I remember shuddering, a tremor of the hand, and for an instant, blinking, I seemed to lose my place in time. I stared down at it, as if it were a scorpion. It was a perfect replica of the telegram I had received forty years earlier. That first one too had come to me at the hands of a student, while enjoying the first few moments of silence after last bell on the last day of school. Nineteen-sixty-five.

Even now, in my study, I steady myself, remembering. *Memory is not always the same as truth.* This, from one of my father's letters. But this year, at age sixty-five, I see myself on the threshold of change. In this dim morning light memories are but a blur. And so it can be. When looking too deeply and too darkly into the past, memory finds it easy to sharpen its hooves on you. It certainly carries no sympathy. And yesterday, it carried none. Sitting at my desk and clearing away books and papers, I opened yesterday's telegram—*Sam. Sorry to inform you of Reuben Flett's death. House fire. Come if you can. Roslyn.*

And so the rain on Francis Street, and on all of Cincinnati this morning, gave me sufficient cause to be awakened. It may just as well be tears. There is no imaginable way of thinking about Reuben without also thinking about Norman Witt, my father. The father I hated. In the great time of the 1940s, my father, along with a Herculean army of citizen soldiers, fought tooth-and-nail against an aggressive enemy bent on defeating the entire world. But even in victory, a beast grew within him, and it was this new enemy that he would wrestle with for the remainder of his days.

Most great heroics go unnoticed. It was in these silent, unheralded battles that my father waged against himself that a horrible myth was allowed to grow. Had I known, even as a child, that I could have been the one to slay that myth; that I could be the one to put a sword into its black heart, I most certainly would have done so. Alas, I did not. I did not because I could not. You see, there is that damnable matter of truth, and truth always makes such a dreadful hero.

Truth is bought with a price. Mine has come like bookends, a telegram on each end. Even now they conjure up a black night, a woman's face in a window, and a land so big and so empty it seemed to fill all of time eternal.

<hr>

It was against the odds of nearly everything that I became a teacher, that a wild boy from the post-war tenements would finish high school, much less be nervy enough to step foot onto a college campus. They weren't even dreams—they were accidents. And, in a sense, escapes. Raised fatherless by a bitter mother, and a peevish sister, I took to the streets early, nickel-and-diming my way through early adolescence like a cat on the prowl.

The sum and total of my father's presence in my life amounted to approximately three weeks in the closing months of 1945, approaching Christmas. I was five, and standing before him at the tiny table wedged up against the wall of our cracker box kitchen, I was looking at a complete stranger. Cincinnati, like so many cities in America, had a section of tenements—project houses—where families settled in, waiting for their soldier-loved-ones to return home from the war. Even by 1940's standards, they were pitifully small, so the kitchen table was the one place where everyone seemed to put down anchor.

Norman Witt had been an early responder to the cry for young men in fighting *the Nazi bastards*, as they were referred to by nearly everybody in those days. And the army wasted no time in snatching him up. By 1942 he was gone, and for the rest of the war, he was in the thick of it, as they say. The closest I ever got to him was watching my mother sitting at that little table, her face shadowed by the dim overhead light, eyes scanning the envelopes containing his letters, as if they were personal affronts against her.

She hated the war, therefore hated him for leaving her to fight in it. Marion Witt took it as a peculiar insult that he would leave her alone with two young children to raise, while he...how did she say it, so he could *cast about like some kind of cavalier*. At four I already had a childish idea of what a cavalier was—Robin Hood, King Arthur—so for a brief time I imagined him a hero. After all, every other father in our neighborhood was off fighting the war too. But my mother's constant grumbling was a sort of propaganda, and being one-sided, was hard to ignore.

Even today, sitting in my study at home, the image of her at that table is as vivid as if she still occupied a place there in the dark. I choose not to conjure her up. But if I wished to, it would be easy enough, the onward march of bitterness deepening year after year in her face and in her attitude. And yet, for the little power she held over me as I was growing up, she managed somehow to bring me into her circle of hatred for the man.

Sergeant First Class Norman Witt was still in uniform when he clambered up the fragmented sidewalk on that leaf-strewn November afternoon, looking peculiarly at every identical unit, trying to find our number 7, poorly painted by the door. My mother saw him from the window, far off, but did not go out to meet him. She had not seen him for over three years, and yet she seethed there in the kitchen, as if she were a kettle simmering on the stove, watching his approach with an odious stare. He smelled of burlap and stale crackers when he came through the door, and dropping his bag on the floor, stepped directly to my mother and kissed her.

She stiffened, receiving it like poison.

The memories are clear.

"Mista Witt, sir," Daisy Ruggles said, her voice barely a sparrow's chirp. She saw me at my desk, her shiny black face, plump as a plum between two pretty ears. "I got this for you," edging closer. Looking up I saw this girl who I just had in fifth period staring at me with wonderful yet respectful curiosity. In her hand was what was easy to recognize—a Western Union telegram—and this being 1965, not so uncommon. Living in the tenements, it was hard not to notice the almost constant ringing of the bicycle-bell of the telegram boy as he peddled nervously through the neighborhood. Even at age three and four, it was a learned thing to know it as an omen of dread for its recipient.

I was seated at my desk at Public School #17, my third year of teaching history to children of the inner-city, which post-war prosperity had seemed to pass over, for one reason or the other. I was halfway finished with my tuna sandwich and nursing a bottle of Coke that had turned lukewarm when Daisy appeared. I always liked this child because there appeared in her face the look of expectant hope. Believing, perhaps, that I held within my teaching knowledge some saving nugget of truth that she might use to better her life. In reality, looking back to that time, I am shamed by my lack of teaching imagination. I taught straight from the text book, which I soon learned, leaves students with a history filled with holes. But it mattered not, for as Daisy Ruggles stood before me, holding the telegram, we both knew it was the last day of the school year, the second of June, and that summer vacation stretched before us both, meaning far different things for each of us.

The difference for me—a difference which extended to the rest of my life—was just then being hand-delivered to me by this charitable angel, Daisy Ruggles. I took the telegram from her but paid no attention to it, instead smiled at her.

"Daisy, do you have plans for this summer?" It was easy to be kind to this girl.

As a known hard-ass in our neighborhood growing up, my hateful ramparts had been bombarded by Ashley Givens, a skinny girl two years younger than me, who first followed me into maddening annoyance before felling me with a kiss. It was from Ashley that I learned that not all women were the same, and that some deserved—truly deserved— any tenderness offered them. Daisy Ruggles was such a woman-child.

"No, Mista' Witt. Jist the same as always." Then, staring at the ceiling for a moment, she said, "Oh, we'll have games in the street. And there's that park. Mama will have lots of chores for me to do too."

"Like washing and ironing clothes?"

Daisy laughed, losing some of her shyness.

"I pretty much know all about that myself, Daisy. When I was your age I developed into a champion ironer."

This made her laugh again, a honeyed laugh that showed her white teeth.

"You are doing really well in history, Daisy. You had no missing assignments. Next year you will be a junior, and I would like to make sure you get in my class again. If you'd like that. I need all the smart students I can get." My turn to laugh. "It makes me look good."

"Oh, I'd like that, Mista' Witt."

Before she left I loaned her a copy of *Never Cry Wolf.*

She held it delicately, as if it were an egg, and said, "Mar-ley Mo-wat. That's an interesting name." She said an interesting name, not a funny name, like so many of her classmates might have said, mockingly. She was nearly breathless receiving it.

"I've read it, Daisy," I said. "I think it might help ease the hot summer for you."

She left like a whisper.

The telegram lay on my desk now and I finished my sandwich without looking at it. Instead, my mind drifted back to my more immediate problem—Mercedes Belfour. Mercedes Belfour, who at that very hour was either lying naked in my bed on my second floor flat, or else taking scissors to my ties. These were her ranges, from a thoroughbred of sexual prowess, to a devil of hair-trigger rage. She was left over from a wolf pack completely foreign to me, of yachts, dinner parties, shopping sprees, drinking binges and spoiled-kitten selfishness. I say left over, for Mercedes was older than my twenty-six by three years, which in her crowd put her between post-debutante and early head-hunter.

We met six months before. She rather liked to call it a rescue. One of those days that doubled for catastrophe when a bad day in the classroom is joined later by one of my dreaded—and dreadful—meetings with my mother. Simeon Stubbs threw a punch at Nick Camoncho because Nick flicked him in the back of the head with a rubber band. Stupid stuff, but Simeon, as I learned later, had experienced a bad day of his own—his family getting evicted from their tenement for delinquent rent. Nick, normally a pretty good kid, was just having fun.

Growing up in the tenements of Cincinnati myself, this altercation was right up my alley. I knew as many ways to escalate as I did to de-escalate such problems. I had earned my scars honestly, if not honorably. Nick received a bloody lip, which served him right, and Simeon an expulsion, which I was able to stay at the last minute once I found out about his home situation. I pleaded his case before the principal, and later, alone in my room after school with Simeon, I allowed him to vent and cry his shame.

"Look at me, Simeon," I said. "For years I was nothing but a puke on the streets of the tenements. A regular piss-willie. But here I am, playing teacher. The tenement was not who I really was. So don't let it define you either."

By the next morning I would feel like a royal hypocrite.

My meeting with Marion Witt, if you can imagine it, was worse, and for her I had no words of wisdom, only silence, followed by anger. Twenty years after my father deserted us, my mother remained steadfast in her bitterness towards him, and her loathsome self-pity over every breath she took. *The son of a bitch.* The glass on the table had a permanent red ring around it where her last glass of cheap wine had dried. It was being filled again as we sat there at the kitchen table—the same kitchen table where she, my sister and I had gathered as a broken family. Marion Witt had not improved her lot by one stitch.

"How's things, Mom?" I was lost for anything meaningful to say.

"You call this a…life? Thaase a…*joke*," her wine slur already apparent. She poured her glass full. "Cleaning up…after…" She took a deep drink. She was going to say, cleaning up after me, but then she caught herself, realizing I wasn't ten anymore. I laid a twenty dollar bill on the table. She nearly choked. With a brush of her hand she swept it off the table and onto the floor. Her voice shrill now. "I…don't need your…damn *charity*." Half standing now she spilled some wine on the knuckles of her hand, which she promptly licked off. Leaving the house, the only satisfaction I gained was knowing the money I had given her would not remain on the floor for long.

My old Ford sedan knew the way to the Red Spot Tavern on 68th, but for some unknown reason—unknown at the time, but years later, as I put events together, more like fate—I spied the lights of the high-rise Red Lion Hotel downtown. It glittered red and yellow in the night as if a wagging finger beckoning me.

I obeyed.

Somewhere, in the early morning distance, I can hear a train whistle. It is leaking into my den through a window that I leave open a crack, rain or shine. Today it is rain, but as I look back on the telegram I received yesterday, informing me of Reuben Flett's death, the sound of this train serves only to fill my head with his image. Above my right eyebrow, a small scar remains from the day this young Colville Indian gave me my first meaningful history lesson. It forced me to become a teacher of history as history truly was, rather than a cookie-cutter regurgitation of important dates that drizzle like the rehearsing of prime factors in a math class. It is not dates on a calendar that equip us to understanding history, it is the events themselves, and more so the chain reaction that sparked those events in the first place. And how they effected the thoughts and actions of men. And women. History is about dominos. Last week, in trying to draw my juniors into understanding this concept, I ordered in Domino's pizza for my sixth-period class. It got their attention.

The sound of this train's whistle seems to be fading eastward. The one I took in the summer of 1965 was traveling in the opposite direction, across the Great Void, as we call it when we study Lewis and Clark. West, because that is where the telegram that Daisy Ruggles gave me instructed me to go. I would rather have not gone at all. But then, there was that matter of Mercedes Belfour.

After Daisy left, I stood at the window taking in the dismal view of a street gone to decay. It would be years before I had the view I now enjoy at Whittier High School. PS #17 found itself wedged in the middle of a lost neighborhood. Several blocks away there were thriving neighborhood grocery stores, drug stores, laundries and Mom and Pop diners, but our school seemed nestled in a pavilion of ruin. What I saw was a fenced-in basketball court where seven or eight boys were starting their summer with a game of ten-point. I could hear the thumping of the ball as it slammed the cracked concrete court and the tremor of it felt too much like my beating heart. So I turned back to my desk and the telegram that awaited me.

Mr. Witt. Sorry to inform you that your father Norman Witt has passed away. His personal effects can be found in Eltopia, Washington where he lived. Trains run Tuesdays & Fridays. Yours, Nancy McGrath, Postmistress.

Well, I thought. There it is—the confirmation. Not so much that he died, but that he ever lived in the first place.

The Red Lion Hotel was out of my class range, even as a teacher. The top two floors were dedicated to entertainment, with a stage, dance floors and bars on each, and designed to fill the desires of partygoers of the yacht clubs, country clubs, lawyers, doctors and the more prominent executives of the city. But my tie and jacket managed to fool the elevator operator, not because I looked important, rather because my eyes were on the floor and I had the woebegone appearance of someone who'd just lost a small fortune in a bad business deal. I looked ticked, because I was. I had saved a kid from being expelled from school, but had no way of helping him live the rest of his life.

I was not a drunk. Far from it. Watching my mother's decline had a clear message written across it. A rare Vodka Collins however could sometimes help erase the clouds of a bad teaching day. Today had been a bad teaching day and regrettably accounted for my second, and then third Vodka Collins.

From the beginning, I had picked the wrong place to unwind. With Simeon still on my mind I stumbled into the top floor bar to find myself in the middle of a debutante bash. Young people were hardly strangers to me, but I was used to underprivileged ones, who would likely consider me a traitor were they to know I even came into close proximity with the "have-it-alls" as they mockingly referred to them. But there I was. So I took a stool at the farthest and darkest corner of the bar.

Here there was no Reds game on the television, because there was no television. The sports bar was on the floor below, the one I had missed. But before me was my first drink, so I stayed. The music was loud and the girls, in their finery, were on the dance floor spinning around in their white dresses, putting a dizzying spin on the whole room. Young men, awkward and long-limbed, followed along like long-toothed wolves, with the acute hunger for conquest. The girls, no doubt rich and spoiled, were likely secreting the same thoughts.

I was not old—twenty-six is not old—and some of these boys were not necessarily boys either, some likely approaching my own age. Through my second Collins, on an empty stomach, I found myself escaping the problems of Simeon and allowing my eyes to settle on the dancing girls. Some of them were unattractive, with only their money—their daddy's money—to help them along the way. But many of them were quite pretty and worth the effort of my study. I was presently living out my days alone, having long ago moved on from Ashley. She would have been a prize had I the sense to know it at the time, but I was young and dumb and filled with false bravado.

This morning, sitting in the quietness of my den, I cannot even remotely recall which young girl it was, or even what she looked like—my third Collins had just arrived—but that she had dark brown hair and the boy she was with had blonde hair, showing the early traces of a Beatles cut. That's it. In fact, even at the time, I doubt I looked into either of their faces. But somewhere in that madding crowd, the girl approached me, having seen me staring, and she unexpectedly kissed me on the mouth. It was like a gunshot, so surprised I was. She had her reasons, half-drunk herself no doubt, from a smuggled bottle in her purse, and the main reason, standing in shock, was her escort, the Beatles haircut kid. Inflicting a jealousy likely emerging out of the Garden of Eden.

I remember watching as the girl disappeared as mysteriously as she had arrived, and in her place came the boy/man. Seeing what was coming I scarcely managed to climb from my stool and we were locked in a close-quarter struggle. Drunk or not, I had the good sense to know that I was a teacher, and if word of this leaked out, I would not be a teacher tomorrow. So I wrapped my arms around his and we spun in a kind of macabre dance. A loud cheer erupted from the young crowd—Romans at the Colosseum—and the two of us, the jealous boy and me, tried to keep our footing. At some point we separated, and in a miracle of reflex I stepped back from one of his foolish haymakers.

Moments like this always come in flashes, like a strobe light. In an instant the boy was gone and I felt myself being dragged away by the collar of my jacket. Bouncers, I thought, and then what—jail? But in my ear came a woman's voice—Mercedes Belfour's voice—*Come along, Sluggo*. And I came along, into the elevator, and the sudden rush of the long descent. Even by that time I couldn't distinguish her face, only her voice, an edge of Alpha Dog—a throaty version of some singer I'd heard on the radio.

Next was the parking lot, and then my car. But I was giving her my keys and I found myself being folded into the passenger seat. Nothing, absolutely nothing, until the next morning when the blinds to my bedroom window were suddenly thrust upward, the winter sun stabbing me in the face. The first thing I saw was this tall, blond-haired woman staring down at me. Her naked breasts showed the healthy heft of cantaloupes and the velvety color of cow's milk with nipples copper brown. When I finally found her face, frozen there was the expression of a conqueror. She might as well have been holding a spear.

There is a book in my study, *The Band of Brothers*, by Stephen Ambrose, one I bought and read in the 90s, where between the pages is tucked the telegram I received back then, about my father's death. This new one, about Reuben, I have decided will be placed beside it. In an odd gesture which means something only to me, I will reunite these two men in a ceremony both ridiculous and deeply felt.

Love is a layered object. Or so I believe. A man can love his dog—I've had several worthy of my love; Freckles, Snickers and Stella—and oftentimes the love a dog will give you back is some of the best you'll ever get. There was a purity to the love I felt for Ashley Given, pure in its adolescent sense. Love was never a presence in our home, so Ashley opened a door, not only previously unopened but highly unknown. Her secret affection towards me was something she harbored long before I knew she even existed. So she confessed. She was just another girl in the neighborhood, until that day when she got glasses to fix her nearsightedness. She instantly became a new person.

"Can I sit by you?"

We were on a city bus, going to I forget where. It was that simple. I nodded and she sat, and for a long moment I puzzled over her. I'd seen her a thousand times, but never this close up. Her glasses made her look...well, smarter for one, but prettier. More noticeable. And her hair, rather an ordinary brown, suddenly smelled like a garden in spring. I had never smelled a girl's hair before. Or never realized it if I had. But Ashley's hair was a bouquet. It took me another minute to realize that there were plenty of empty seats on the bus, but she'd asked to sit by me.

I was eighteen and she was fifteen and nothing that ever happened between us for the time we spent together was regrettable. Even today. As a young tough on the streets of the tenements, full of anger and hate, Ashley turned a dial on my heart that would eventually take me to my knees. To be loved by anyone, much less a sweet young girl, was beyond anything I could have ever imagined, much less hoped for. Her kisses were explorative and inexperienced, and my bravado melted under them.

I speak of Ashley Given now to draw a stark contrast to Mercedes Belfour. From the moment of my *rescue*, I became the property of Mercedes. And because of her body, and the freedom with which she shared it, my captivity was a welcome thing. For a while. She had money and I had nothing, save for my teaching career, which wasn't really a career yet, not at that point. Just a job. But a job I needed, and foolishly thought I was good at. Words like bipolar or manic-depressive weren't part of the everyday medical jargon in the nineteen-sixties. But looking back, it was clear that I was joined in lust with a mad woman.

Behind my self-defined toughness hid a terrified young man. Every fight I had ever gotten into in the neighborhood to prove my street corner rule had all been fought because of fear—fear of discovery. I trembled at a future I feared had no purpose. I was, and I knew it, a fatherless nobody. The kids in my tenement blocks had different kinds of fathers. Some came back from the war better men than when they left. Some loved their wives and children like never before. Others came back haunted by what they'd seen and done in the war. Oftentimes these fathers became ghosts to who they once were. And then there were the fathers that never came back at all, having been killed in North Africa or France or Germany. Even Italy. The pain of that was visible on every face in those families, until one day they realized that there was a certain kind of honor in their loss. And so they hung on to that. My father came back, but left again, never to be seen again. At least, not by me.

Mercedes must have seen my fear and the self-hatred it had bored into me and decided I was someone easy to control. And she'd been right. At least at first. But a steady diet of even the sweetest fruit gets old after a while. She had her own apartment across town, in a much dignified neighborhood—dignified being her word—but was always waiting for me in my slum apartment as soon as I got home from school. Looking back, and knowing better now how her brain must have worked, I think she found my apartment so beneath her that it became a turn-on. Something akin to making love in a barn—base and animal-like but deliciously wicked.

In public, when Mercedes and I were out somewhere, she always made sure I had the proper clothes. Knowing my shirt and pants size, she would shop while I was working and when I came home she'd spring new clothes on me that fit perfectly but made me feel like a society ape, someone she was hoping to recreate. I protested but she'd tell me she didn't want to be seen with a clod. She arranged barber appointments for me, and bought me new ties. But after months of her possessiveness and control, an incident happened that sowed the seeds of my discontent.

Jewelry was a fixation with her. There were occasions, when we were having sex—making love did not then, or now, seem an appropriate definition—when she would be totally naked and yet have an expensive necklace swinging in front of me, swaying back and forth like a crazed pendulum on a clock. *You need something fancy*, she'd said. *Something with class. A ring. Yes, a nice, big, fat ring.* So, by week's end, and with one of her yacht parties circled on her calendar, I found myself standing with her at an upscale jeweler's.

"I'm not really a jewelry kind of guy."

"I'm going to buy you a ring so stop arguing."

She had the clerk show her a black onyx with a single diamond in the center.

"Here," she said. "Try this on. See if it fits."

It was too small and I was relieved because it was flashy and garish and everything I was not.

"Well, I like it," she said, "and the jeweler can size it for you."

"Did you see the price?"

"Twenty-five hundred. So?"

"I refuse to have that ring. I don't like it and it's too expensive anyway."

I already knew that Mercedes Belfour was of the Chicago Belfours, who owned a string of investment firms, all with different names, and that because Daddy Belfour had never been able to unload his daughter on one of Chicago's lackey bachelors during her debutante years, he would have to settle for giving her whatever she wanted. And on that day she wanted me to have a ring.

Our argument went back and forth, until suddenly, to the shock of both me and the clerk, she slapped me hard across the face. "You're getting a ring. You bastard. You belong to me and you're getting a ring. This ring," she screamed, pointing at the ugly thing.

My face burned, from the slap and from humiliation. Self-humiliation. How had I come to this place? And yet, that night, as we sat across from each other on my small dining table, eating take-out

Chinese food, she was a lamb. She'd cried over something—I don't remember what—and here then I saw a carbon copy of myself. A scared, angry child. And somehow all the money in the world, which she felt she had, couldn't put Mercedes Belfour back together again. I knew then that I would be leaving her, even though I had no idea when or how.

Then came the last day of school, and the telegram announcing my father's death. Inwardly I had no desire, or intention, of going out to Washington State to retrieve the worthless belongings of a man I hated. It would be an insult to everything I had been led to believe about myself. But as I sat in my classroom on that warm June day in 1965, I saw my opening.

History, as I've said, isn't just a glob of separate events, shoved together to fit in a text book. Rather, it is a thread; a thread with knots. There are knots showing the American Revolution and the Constitution; knots that show the Alamo or the Trail of Tears or the individual battles of the Civil War, like Gettysburg. There are many knots but they are still all connected to each other. Before going to Eltopia, I never realized this. I was young and dumb and had the ridiculous idea that the authors of school history books knew things beyond my understanding.

On my return from Eltopia, I immediately went to the hardware store and bought a ball of twine, and on that twine I started tying knots—many knots—and then I strung that thread of twine across the ceiling of my classroom from one wall to the other. Here then, I told my students, is history. It's all connected.

Mercedes watched me pack my suitcase. She stood in her favorite wardrobe of pure, uncovered flesh. Her arms were at her side and I noticed her fingers were puzzling with themselves, the way the movies always portrayed a gunslinger before a gunfight. She hadn't shown anger, only a vague sadness, as if she had already seen this before, not with me but with many other men. It was even over in her own mind and she'd decided it—or that I—wasn't worth the fight. As her hands came up to touch her own breasts, I felt a sudden sadness of my own. The dragon was a lamb again, with a heart and a memory. The telegram laid on the dresser, a talisman noting our end.

That there was no fight, no screaming or clinging, I wondered if perhaps she might have been seeing someone, or several someones, and was as ready for this detachment as much as me. For a moment it threw a shock of jealousy through me. The thought of sharing this sex-animal with someone else made me question this whole idea of leaving her. But she just stood there, watching me throw a few shirts—shirts she'd bought me—into my old suitcase, along with toiletries and a book. I believed, at that moment, that Mercedes knew that she was a wreck, and that whatever lay ahead for her, it would be a repeat of this—another rescue of someone.

"I'll go with you," she said. "If you want."

Here it was, the line in the sand. The Colonel Travis moment—are you with me or not?

Instead of saying anything, I said nothing.

Mercedes had a key of course, so when I returned, in a week, in a month, in a thousand years, I was sure her things would be gone from my apartment.

It had taken Ashley Given a little longer to get into college. Her father had returned from the war a changed man; changed for the better, and working hard was able to sacrifice his own betterment for the sake of his lovely daughter. In my apartment, with Mercedes still standing naked but wordless in the kitchen, I gave her one last kiss and then left. And then, as if living through some kind of strange death, I took a bus to where Ashley now lived, out of the tenements at last. I knocked on the door and when she saw me she leapt into my arms. I believe I could have married her there on the spot. I could have tied a knot in my own thread of history and likely would have been both happy and loved. But I didn't. Instead I told her where I was going and why. She was already seeing a fellow from school, I'd heard that, and my offer of marriage might have been turned down anyway, but I just needed to see the face of someone I knew was real. It happens sometimes, since life is a strange place to call home. And we do things, not often enough, that give us peace. Ashley at that moment, was my peace, because where I was going, and what I would do there, would be the most frightening thing I'd ever done, before or since. She had new glasses, and she kissed me in that old familiar way.

In my study now, remembering, I understand better about those layers of love. A dog, yes. Ashley. Mercedes. My wife is my universal love. She knows me and thinks, at least, that she has me figured out. Like me, she is a teacher. Our years together have produced two wonderful children, Rex, who is doing things with computers I'll never understand, and Colette, who is married with children.

I am holding the telegram that notified me of Reuben Flett's passing. He was a man, in 1965, at the end of a long train ride, I would soon meet. The scar above my eye throbs sometimes, and it is throbbing this early morning, with rain out my window. But it is a throbbing of love, high on its many layers.

My name is Sam Witt. Not Samuel, just Sam. Sam Benjamin Witt, with some loose but unexplained connection to a distant uncle. My dead father was Norman Witt, with no middle name. My mother, Marion Witt was once Marion Benson, daughter of an Ohio farmer who lost his life under the wheels of a tractor when she was only ten. She rarely spoke of him, and never of her mother. Such, it seems, is the way of embittered people. My mother, Marion, may have been born bitter, long before she ever met my father. That, of course, is only a guess. In spite of it, they produced two children, my older sister, Shirley, who is now Shirley Hicks, an indelicate shrew with a browbeaten husband and one daughter, once pitiful but no longer, who, when she turned eighteen, escaped and now lives happily with a decent man in Georgia.

And then there was me.

This is the long way of getting to the point. It turned out that the book I absently threw in my suitcase while the naked Mercedes stood watching, was Charles Webb's, *The Graduate*, whose main character was

Benjamin. Benjamin Braddock. It seemed funny at the moment, and remains funny to this day, that I found a wealth of similarities between Benjamin Braddock and Sam Benjamin Witt. Both directionless messes. Indeed, Mercedes Belfour was not the same age as Mrs. Robinson in the book, she was still an older, and much more experienced woman than any I'd ever had a chance to bed.

I knew nothing of the West, capital *W*, except what I'd learned in college, which wasn't much, in spite of being a history major, and from the glib text books we were forced to buy. Instead of *The Graduate*, I might have bettered my knowledge by reading something by Zane Grey or Louis L'Amour where the land often became the main character. Grey had actually written a book called, *The Desert of Wheat*, which takes place in Washington State during World War I. But I didn't discover that until later, after I had returned to Cincinnati, where I began reading Zane Grey novels with something approaching a vengeance.

But Benjamin Braddock was lost, and so was I, and he made agreeable company for my train ride into the unknown. There were times though, once the night train became a day train and the sun came up over Iowa when I realized I was in an altogether new country. We chugged along, a caterpillar of train cars, winding through wheat fields, hay fields and corn fields, a dust-reddened sun reminding me of poems I'd read by Carl Sandburg, who had come from such a place as this and knew how to capture its barren beauty in his hundreds of poems. He knew how to extract the honey from the husk.

In truth, I'd never been on a train before. The whole idea of it never really sank in until we were plunged into the night and the lights of Cincinnati faded in the distance. Even the millions of lights of Chicago would be passed in the night, giving me the impression of entering into a kind of space travel. But the sun and Iowa brought me back to earth, and the reason for this trip suddenly shown as bright as the day out the window, and the fear returned. It was real fear, for I was going to the place where my father had settled, over two thousand miles from his family. I envisioned that this place, Eltopia, as a backwater town peopled by hicks. I would hold to that impression for the first twelve hours I was there. It didn't last though.

But the image of Mercedes' tits and ass stayed with me, and at times I was fully tempted to disembark somewhere and jump the first return train back to her. Such is the powerful grip of lust. I was a fool and the sad thing was, I knew I was a fool. A weak, disgusting fool. I finished *The Graduate* and hungered for another book, another magazine, another anything to take my mind off of her.

I found myself falling victim in conversation to a man traveling home to Omaha, who had been in New York to bury a brother. The brother, it turned out, had been a twin, and the man—he introduced himself as Tom—made a great declaration of being only half alive now, having lost his other half. He was a nice man in his forties, and I certainly felt bad for his circumstances, but he was so overwhelmed with facing the world now as just that one person that I felt a hypocrite. I was on a similar mission, to bury my father, in a sense, and yet all I could think about was the smooth skin and lips of a woman I'd left behind. But Tom loved his brother, and me, I hated my father.

My wife has always had an affection for craftsman houses. When we were married I was still teaching at PS #17 and would be for another two years. After leaving there I taught at another public school, number 38—strange, as there were not thirty-eight such schools in Cincinnati, their numbers had more to do with districts and voting townships and such. My wife was teaching by that time too and my time and confidence at these PS schools gave me the courage to apply for a history position at Whittier, a dream school, as I was told by the principal during the interview. The way education goes, there are very few dream schools, and most schools of any kind have the same fate of decline if not kept to high standards. I got myself in trouble early when they found out I'd voted for Ronald Reagan. The teacher's union, even then, was in bed with the Democrats.

But in time I would become respected, by the students first and the staff later, and found myself applying for and winning the job of coaching a floundering baseball team. I had coached some at PS

17 and 38, mostly for the extra money, but the baseball Staggs of Whittier High School had fallen short of late by the so-called dream school standard. My first year was hardly better, but we managed to improve year by year and in the eighties we earned two trips to the state championships, winning both times. A trophy naming me Coach of the Year rests on a shelf before me right now, among other things in my study. There are photographs of those winning teams, and several signed baseballs by my players.

I had played college ball for two years, at first a catcher, and then a first baseman. But my desire to coach had nothing to do with that. It was, instead, an act of sheer determination, put forth in an unspoken challenge by the Indian, Reuben Flett. All of that, and much more, awaited me in Eltopia, with a crippling heartbreak nearly too enormous to measure.

But with both my wife and I teaching, we could finally look for and find our craftsman house. The neighborhood isn't what it once was, back in the twenties and thirties, but it remains better than most, and it is close to both our schools. The move from our former neighborhood was a boon for the children as it gave both Rex and Colette the opportunity to attend our respective schools, my wife's middle school, Granger, and my Whittier. In fact, I had the double pleasure—or is it a triple pleasure—to coach Rex on my baseball team, and to watch Colette play on the girls' basketball team, unfortunately and curiously named the Staggettes.

Yesterday afternoon, when Olive Nettles brought me this, my second telegram, with Reuben's name staring back at me like a damaged star, I confess I walked to the window of my classroom, and looking down on the empty practice field, I wept. They were jolting tears, the kind that carry years with them, coming from a place far deeper than the gut. They come from a broken heart. I grieved for my friend, but I also grieved for myself, my once young but now older self. Young people never get it till they themselves arrive there. When you are young, you wake up with your life in front of you. When you get older, like me, you wake up with your day in front of you. Nothing more. Here, at that moment, was my life's portion—a vacated baseball practice field where

I once ruled; a sixty-fifth birthday, seven weeks earlier; and shelves of dog-eared text books, equaling a life of tying knots in the twine of my history. And then this—not a death by old age, or a slow illness. Not even a death by sudden heart attack. But Reuben's death by a house fire. A terrifying death by Hell's fire.

I have not seen Reuben for nearly five years. In the past, as a family, we had gone back to Eltopia for visits, and this year it was on the books. A July trip where Reuben and I could sit around and smoke cigars and drink cold Rainier beers and talk about old times. It's what young people turning older do. We were going to visit some places, known only to us and a few others. In one of Reuben's letters he had said that the old wooden wheat warehouses had been torn down and replaced with concrete ones, forcing the little town to lose some of its charm. And that the Amtrak, still running from Spokane through Ritzville heading south, no longer stopped at Eltopia now, though sometimes as a dedicated ritual. The old school still stands, and is well cared for, even though kids no longer go there, instead taking buses to Mesa or Pasco. They use the school for weekly Farmers Markets and holiday dances. Things change.

In my classroom, spent by my weeping, I thought of where he might be buried, or if he had been left unburied, waiting for a funeral, a funeral my wife and I will attend. Our plane leaves Cincinnati today and will arrive in Spokane by early afternoon. If I have any say in the matter, I hope to have Reuben buried—what is left of him, in his involuntary cremation—in that secret place. It is where he belongs. It is where my heart belongs.

We packed last night, working through another round of tears. It's no wonder I couldn't sleep. Rain or no rain, I might have awakened anyway. The ghost of my father, as I think of him, always arrives with the rain. He comes with the snow too. And though I try my best to teach deep into American history, presenting the Battle of the Bulge is hard to replicate with mere words. It needs rifle shots. It needs grenades and artillery. It needs the screams of the dying. It deserves everything I want to give it but cannot.

History is boring. I've heard this a thousand times from

unimaginative students.

Then you are boring, I retort.

Hey! I'm not boring.

If history is boring than you are boring...because, you are, this very moment, living history. Therefore, if history is boring, then you are boring as well.

But...

By virtue of the fact you are breathing air at this moment in time, makes you part of a continuous history. Not just your own personal history, but the part you may or may not play in this country's history. Even your dying can leave a mark on history, depending on how and when that might happen. If I can do my job properly, you likely will not die of boredom.

The following silence is painful because it has required this dumbass kid, and others like him, to actually think.

I am secretly ashamed to say, that it took Eltopia for even me to understand this.

Cincinnati is a city of rivers and much can be made of them, the Ohio River being principal among them. But the Whitewater River, the Little Miami and the Great Miami rivers, as well as the Licking River all claim territory in or near my city. But even as a wet-behind-the-ears history teacher in my early days of teaching at P.S. 17, I had fumbled my way through a section on the Lewis and Clark Expedition, trying to form a visual picture for my students. After returning from Eltopia, I saw this effort for what it was—an utter failure.

In what some would consider an enormous wasteland, so barren it could be the surface of a distant planet, that great vacant swath of eastern Washington is sliced down the middle by the colossus of the west, the immense Columbia River, carving itself through deep basalt cliffs and gorges until it spills into the Pacific Ocean, which has never been pacific. This, and scores of mighty amphitheaters of natural beauty awaited me. I thought I knew rivers. I knew nothing.

And though into this world the train carried me, I was concerned only with my present predicament. Who was this postmistress, Nancy McGrath? Why was she the one to notify me, and not a doctor or a coroner? What do I say when I get there? And what kind of personal effects could I ever care about that belonged to the father who abandoned me? Staring out the window at Iowa, I declared I would stay only long enough to throw his junk in the garbage and get back on the train for home. Maybe Ashley Given would give up her new boyfriend for me, and she and I could settle into a happy life.

The man, Tom, who lost his twin brother, detrained in Omaha, his grief so upon him he was bent and sorrowful looking, and could have passed for a hundred-year-old. It was a forty-minute layover so I followed him into the terminal to see if he had any family meeting him there. I felt the need to say something to him, something comforting, but what the hell did I know about comfort. I wasn't wise enough yet to understand that sometimes no words are better than the wrong words. But following him, I saw that he seemed preoccupied with his wristwatch. He kept checking it, as if whoever was to meet him was late.

Coming up behind him, I said, "I could use a coffee, Tom. Care to join me?"

I was certain he would decline, but was surprised when he didn't.

Nodding, he said, "Coffee sounds fine. There's a diner down the street."

In 1965 I was notoriously selfish. Even what seemed like a thoughtful gesture had much more to do with my own needs. I was tired of wearing my brain out with what lay ahead of me, and as much about what I had just left behind. True, I wanted coffee, and I wanted company, for a while at least. And I secretly figured that chatting with a man living out his misery just might make my own dilemma seem less a burden. Even as we sat in a booth at the diner I felt like a blackguard.

"Tim. That was my brother's name. Tim and Tom. A mother's revenge." He said it in a funny way, his sarcasm the first sign of something deeper in the man. His voice seemed to even out as he talked, speaking of their years growing up in a small town west of Omaha, where every star in the sky can be seen at night, all the way to the second and third heaven. And the aurora borealis, which, like an elusive young woman, shows herself on those rare nights when she waves her skirts in her enticing way. And at night, with the windows open, you can hear the music of frogs in the field, and the crickets, and the smell of fresh mown alfalfa is more sensual than the perfume of a goddess.

My coffee turned cold listening to this man. In my entire life I had never heard anybody talk with such eloquence about the things dear to them. Or of the land. His brother's death was his present concern, but it did not appear to conquer his other passions, or kill the knowledge that beauty remained, out there, apart from his grief. The little poetry I had read by that time was nothing compared to this man's expressiveness; this man's love for things entirely beyond me. Frogs? Alfalfa? If he loved this wild country as much as this, it was no wonder he had loved his brother more. And that too was beyond me. Here, sitting before me, sat a man torn to shreds on the inside by the death of his twin, and yet he had saved a place in his heart—a holy place—for the land and the things that were kept there, waiting for his return. A grieving man who I'd taken for a delicately fragile mess, had proven himself the opposite. I beat against a sick kind of jealousy for Tom being a better man than me.

It set me thinking about the layers of love again, and wondering if the feeling I had for Ashley Givens had ever approached actual love. When Tom's wife arrived, a comely woman in a yellow and green sundress, he embraced her warmly. Then he shook my hand and wished me well. I watched them leave, afraid that if I moved at all, I might crumble like a pillar of salt.

———

By afternoon there were heat shimmers on the open land outside the train's window. I might as well have been traveling through Hungary or Morocco, as strange as this all was to me. Distant tractors working in the fields, black smoke chuffing from their stacks; perfectly lined windrows of hay looking like some difficult geometry puzzle;

silos rising against the sky, as if fortresses against enemy invaders; and everywhere cows and horses, some fenced and some free, some with riders, hats blowing off in the wind. I almost giggled to myself from sheer realization that this too was America.

Eventually the land became the same and I dozed, giving Mercedes a chance to reenter my thoughts. Her college degree from the University of Chicago had been in art history. She was a dedicated follower of Degas and in our better hours she plied me with books containing his paintings, flipping the pages back and forth to help me get a feel for the man, not just the artist. *One needs to have been sad and serious for a longtime to enjoy oneself so much.* She said this in such a casual way that I thought at first they were Mercedes' own words, but it turned out they were Degas' notes from a journal he kept in his later years. It was just that Mercedes had memorized them so well they had become her own.

Sad and serious? I wondered if that was a dim window into her fractured personality. Further, after turning page after page of Degas' nudes, I wondered if Mercedes had not, in some unexplored alleyway of imagination, dreamt herself into believing she was one of his models. One of her favorite paintings was *The Bath*, which showed a woman stepping into a bathtub, her rumpled bed in the foreground. Mercedes laid open the book to that painting and told me to study it. She then led me into the bathroom where she made a surprisingly incisive replication of it, left leg in the tub, right leg at mid-step, right arm and hand on the tub's rim, and her generous breasts hanging loosely from her bent form. She held that pose long enough for me to study it—study her—and applaud her effort.

Mercedes had studied for a year in Europe, primarily in France and Italy, touring the grand museums and cathedrals. She was no stranger to the works of Renoir and Monet and Pissarro and Bouguereau, but it was Edgar Degas' work that had won her heart. *He offers me with an excuse,* she once said. Waiting for her to expound, and seeing my raised eyebrow, she said, *to be both voyeur and exhibitionist.* She then pointed to the painting, *The Young Spartans,* which portrayed a group of naked young men squaring off in a grassy field against a group of bare-breasted young women. Adding a degree of shock to the scene shows a group of Victorian women, fully dressed in long gowns and hats in the background watching, in either delight or disgust, at this erotic display of nakedness. *Here I can be either a lascivious watcher or a lascivious show off. Either way, it's sexual.*

I soon realized I had bridled myself with a forest nymph, as in nymphomaniac. But I also knew that a steady diet of anything gets old, and in Mercedes case, connecting herself with Degas paintings added something deeper to her...to her what? Her problem. For most of my enslavement to her, I did not see it as a problem. The sex was never bad, and so new to me that I didn't complain. It was her unpredictable outrages. As they say, everything goes back to the bedroom, and so too did the ebbing and rising tides of her emotions.

I had read a story once about a man who'd been bitten by a rabid raccoon. Lying next to her in bed one night, I dreaded that whatever had possessed Mercedes Belfour might be contagious and I began fearing for my life.

Perhaps these thoughts were brought on by the horses in the Nebraska prairie land, as Degas was rather enamored with horses as a good deal of his sketches gave the strong-legged creatures a prominent place of honor. Or maybe it was just that word, *lascivious*, a word that is hard to shake from a sleepy traveler's mind.

At that moment in time, Reuben Flett did not exist, not yet. And the scar over my right eyebrow had not become a part of my handsome features either. All that was further down the west bound rail line. But in hindsight, which is sometimes both unreliable and usually inaccurate, as memory can often become more fictionalized to suit our dignity, I might have given this adventure the name of one of poet Anne Sexton's books, *To Bedlam and Part Way Back*. The part-way-back would come at the Eltopia train stop as I prepared to return to Cincinnati. I felt I had been through a threshing machine. Everything I thought I had ever known about my father, my mother, and even myself, had been thrown into such a strange light, that I am surprised I had the command of my wits to just stop.

Stop. Had I not, it might have been bedlam and *all* the way back.

The rain is still falling outside my study but it is a good rain. Good because it allows me to be in a thousand different places at once. The picture of my wife that sits on my desk shows her sitting at a table in a brilliant white blouse. Before her, and in contrast, are two arrangements of potted orange and yellow flowers, as well as a glass pitcher of water with lemon slices floating inside. Her hair is not long the way it was when I met her, but still a beautiful brown, with blue eyes the color of a morning sea. They are the eyes I always seek when I am struggling with my footing. They are the eyes, and eventually the words she speaks, of good fellowship and good help.

It is my wife, the middle school English teacher, who furnishes me with helpful anecdotes from the many novels she reads, which she manages to weave into a sort of parallel study of my own varying circumstances. Even this morning, before I crept from our bed, she said in a whisper, *You see…the storm is already dying down.* This is one of her favorite lines she feeds me whenever she knows I am overtaxing my brain and my emotions. I know by now that it is from Colette's *The Ripening Seed*, but it might as well belong solely to my sweet wife, as it comes often enough that it almost serves as a mantra. Funny thing, she claims to have hated that book though I know she has secretly recommended it to a few of her overcharged eighth grade girls who are struggling with their own ripening seeds.

The whole thought of this outlandish book brings something else to mind. The girl character in the story is named Vinca, which is the botanical name for the blue Periwinkle flower, a shorter version of the Russian word *pervincha*. So, tossing this image of girls and Russian together, I am able to arrive at how I came to discover my interest in history. That too was a rainy day and there was no better place to both ride out the storm and to evade the wrath of Marion Witt than the neighborhood library.

Further, I had recently been in a fight with Billy Kendall and knew from the word on the street that his older brother, Ricky Kendall was on the hunt for my blood. Ricky Kendall was a notorious bully and though his little brother, Billy, had left no mark on me in our fight, Ricky had a reputation for *going-for-the-eyes*. I had seen this myself as a spectator once and wondered, while watching, how best I might beat him without losing an eyeball or two. In my mind I had formulated a strategy, but on this rainy day I simply wasn't in the mood to test my theory.

The library, housed in an old building with worn out furniture, had three floors and my favorite spot was in a dimly lit corner where a long table was shoved up close to the radiator, and on this day a rain-streaked window. I could find a book, lay it open on the table, lay my head down, and sleep. If a librarian ever came up to the third floor, which was rare, they'd likely not disturb me since I had, after all, been reading a book. All was gray outside and there were no other people close by, and why would there be, since it was the history section. And every kid, even me at that time—I was sixteen—knew that history was dead.

On that day, though, I didn't need to find a book to do my fake reading because there was already one on the table. And it was already open. I sat down, turned the book toward me and looked upon the page. There, in glossy black and white, stood four beautiful girls. Ashley and I had only barely discovered each other, but by that time I was a young, horny Spartan of my own making. These girls were gorgeous. I looked down at the caption. Romanov. Olga. Tatiana. Maria. Anastasia. I was transfixed. Turning the page brought me horrified to my feet. A picture of a blood-soaked floor and a bullet-riddled wall in a basement in Ekaterinburg, Russia.

I sat back down, disbelieving. No such thing could have happened to such beautiful girls. No animal, no human beast could have looked into those innocent faces and...what? Murdered them. I still remember the bile rising in my throat. Russia. Of course, Russia, where all bad things happened. There and in Germany. I did know that much. I turned to the first page and began reading. I don't remember going downstairs and checking the book out at the front desk, or falling asleep in my bed reading it. It is lost to memory. Only that it happened, and my severe indignation and heartbreak—yes, I might have loved someone as beautiful as these girls—made me shrink under the knowledge of such a horrific act of savagery. I felt my young cheeks bathed in the tears of sudden awareness.

From that day on, well into my college years, the third floor of the neighborhood library, with its rows upon rows of old history books, became my new temple of learning. It became my Smithsonian of research. No matter what came after, Sherman's March to the sea; the sinking of the Lusitania; the beheading of Marie Antoinette; the Lost Battalion of WWI; nothing then, or even now, came close to the indignant massacre of those four enchantingly beautiful Romanov sisters. Never more than at that moment did I wish I could be a time-traveler. I would plot for hours, sometimes even days, preoccupied with how I might alert the Tsar to his impending danger and rescue the entire family. And maybe even marry Tatiana, as she was the most beautiful.

And so it wasn't Abraham Lincoln or Davy Crockett that yanked on my ear, sending me down the path of history, and eventually a history teacher, rather it was a distorted and strangely unhealthy lust for four young girls I could not save from history's evil stroke. Yet, with all of that passion, it still took Eltopia to show me the way to teaching what I felt so deeply.

I bought that book about the Romanovs, and many more like it, and they line the many built-in shelves in my study. Looking out though the window to the somber-soaked streets of Francis and Morris, I realize we will have to take umbrellas if we are to make it to the taxi when that time comes. Whenever we fly, we take a cab for pure convenience. It's more economical then paying for parking for a week at the airport. But that's hours away yet. It's early, and I have things I want to think about.

As it worked out, my strategy against Ricky Kendall never came to fruition. Shortly after falling in love and grief with the doomed Romanov sisters, some Italian kid from another neighborhood, avenging a sister Ricky had gotten too familiar with, beat Kendall so badly that he left town and joined the Navy. The last anybody heard, he was on a ship heading to the Azores.

Darkness is a breeder of ghosts.

A man from the dining car comes forth with a tray of cigarettes and candy bars, a quarter for the candy, fifty cents for the smokes. I fish out a quarter and buy a Hershey bar. The last traces of sun coming through a west window, cast a peach-colored glow around the man's head and it reminds me of seeing my father standing on the sidewalk outside our tenement house in one of the few memories I have of him. It is the same back-cast glow, as if he is an angel. But already, from the hateful words of my mother, he has become a false angel, one I am learning to hate. Such is the crime of propaganda.

I know the way things are going now. The discontented. It is like any steady diet, be it seafood or enchiladas. Daily a person begins to protest against even our better angels. I saw it start when some of my friends returned home from Vietnam in the late sixties and early seventies. The propagandists—the news media, the universities, the hate-baiters—somehow were able to portray the GIs that fought in that war as the real enemies of the state. I was already out of college by then, and teaching, but I saw it and didn't understand it. Some of the boys from my neighborhood who came home to that bitter reception, didn't understand it either. And I was too green of a teacher to know how to articulate it into an object lesson.

So, today, many young people emerging from the halls of higher education, are already tired of a steady diet of freedom; of free enterprise; of tolerance, of opportunity, and because of this bloating of such a diet, they search and seek for something worse. *We have found the enemy, and the enemy is us.* It derives from a lack of original thought. It is too painful to become one's own person so they trade individuality for the soul of a lemming, who will fall for the next cry to race off the cliff. God help us.

And even now, I am confused—am I in my study or am I on the train.

My college baseball career was anything but spectacular. But catchers, then and now, are hard to come by so when my coach, who was also my PE teacher recruited me, I did what I always did, I stumbled blindly down the road of obedience. I admitted I had played B-squad ball in high school as a first basemen, it was Coach Burl Cave, in college, watching my angry determination in running, jumping, boxing, and flag football that put the thought in his head.

"Do you know anything about what a catcher does?" he asked as he walked me towards the locker room after class.

"Some," I said.

"Look, Witt, there's no point sugar-coating it. We lost five seniors from the team at graduation last year. One of them was Cookie Bryant, our catcher, and another was Pete Dirks, the backup catcher."

"I've never played catcher."

"I know. I looked at your high school records. And I know your old coach. Mabry. He said some strange things about you. Frankly, that you were one pissed-off kid. That if you weren't so determined to self-destruct, he would have played you more. He said he even once considered moving you to catcher, but he didn't like your attitude."

We were at the door to the field house now but Coach Cave stopped and put his hand on my shoulder. "We've started pre-season drills. Running, throwing. All that stuff. I'll give you till tomorrow to decide. But if you do, I want you to be my catcher."

"But..."

"Never mind. All you got to do is two things. Squat your ass down behind the plate and catch the ball. And the other is throwing runners out trying to steal second. I've seen you throw. You have a good arm. Your aim sucks, but we'll figure that out as we go."

"What about giving the signs to the pitcher?"

"Never mind that. I'll give the pitcher his signs from the dugout."

He opened the door for me, but before I had even made a move he said, "Oh, by the way. We are baseball people. It's September. We workout from now until our first game in the spring. Nothing too serious to begin with, but we do a lot of running. And I know you can do that. But, listen, Witt, I have some money to burn. Scholarship money. If you get your ass in shape and play hard for me, I think I can help you out with your tuition."

Burl Cave was a con man. He had saved the best for last. No kick-around kid from the tenements with an empty bag of promise would say no to that. And only a con man coach would know how to work the angles. He needed a catcher and he had just bought one.

Up to that time I had been holding down two jobs to scrap out money for my schooling. Back in high school I had worked for the E-Z Auto Parts store as a delivery driver. I'd started out stocking shelves in the back room, putting parts in their allotted slots by parts number, AC-2-W4 where all AC-2-W4 radiator caps went, and so on, until I had numbers galloping through my sleep. One day, when the delivery driver called in sick, and the front counter was too busy to spare a man, the manager said, *Witt, get these batteries over to Humboldt Trucking. Out by the interchange.* I stared at him dumbly. *I don't have a driver's license*, I said. He gave me a look. *I don't give a rat's ass if you have two glass eyes. I want these batteries to Humboldt, and you've got ten minutes to get them there.* And so it went.

The other job was on weekends, washing dishes at the Bay Street Restaurant on the banks of the Little Miami. I made peanuts, but it was bus money for getting back and forth, plus a meal a night, which was not a bad bargain since they specialized in Italian dishes, emphasis on seafood, so it wasn't like a lousy hamburger and fries deal. And on Sunday nights, after work, Casey, the chef, always plied me with leftovers to take home. Sometimes there was so much I gave some to Ashley, which did not hurt my relationship with her father. At home, my mother was closing in on a steady diet of cigarettes and wine, so she only picked at what she felt were *uppity handouts*. And my sister, Shirley, by then had duped poor Stanley Hicks into marriage, so she was master of her own life.

And so I did as Coach Cave asked me. I squatted behind home plate for two years, catching the ball the pitcher threw at my glove, and throwing out runners trying to steal second. It only took me a couple of weeks to realize that this was the best way to learn something new— just get in there and do it, always focusing on success, and never failure. Because of Saturday games I gave up the job at Bay Street, and once the scholarship kicked in, I was able to reduce my hours at E-Z Auto Parts. I still needed spending money, and by then, it was a cinch job. I never did get my driver's license, not until I graduated from college.

Coach Cave gave me something I had never had before, a father figure. He gave me more with the scholarship money, but it was the way he had seen something in me; young, angry, invisible me. He drank a lot I heard, and it might have been what killed him in the end, but it was my first real lesson in the sweetness that can reside in even the most haunted of men. Burl Cave, like my father, Norman Witt, had fought the Germans in Italy, where he was wounded. The horrors he brought home in 1943 did not interfere with his job as a college coach and teacher, only what came in the solitude of his lonely life at home. By the summer of 1965, I would learn a great deal more about haunted men, of which I myself was among the ranks.

Glimpses of North Dakota came as darkness settled over the plains. Our progress was slow and steady, as our train made a northward curve into Minnesota and then turned west again, stopping in Minneapolis/St. Paul, and again in Fargo for layovers. I stretched my legs each time, grabbing food where I could at places that were open late and catered to the rail lines. By first light we were past Bismarck and in Teddy Roosevelt's Badland country. I stared at the strange rock formations embedded in the red earth, and at my first sight of buffalo and wild horses. I clung to the window's edge like a ten year old, but not necessarily with affection, but something closer to mortification. *People actually live out here?* I thought. *It's so barren. How do they exist without tall buildings and a highway system?*

My budget had not only been too slim to afford a sleeping car, the entire planning for this trip took a total of scarcely an hour, much of that time coddling with the odd emotions of Mercedes. It had basically been a snap decision, and so once I left my apartment and took a cab to the train station, I was moving in a stiff, robotic state. And now, entering into my second night of traveling through an emptiness of darkness and landscape, lit only by the moon and stars, I was becoming less interested in what passed beyond my window and more concerned with what lay ahead. If Eltopia was as desolate as this, it would simply add to the puzzle of why my father left Ohio for a wild land of tumbleweeds and blowing wind.

It is now, in my study, with the gray rain pushing and pulling at my heart, that another of my wife's forced lessons sifted through from her unique knowledge of the written word, this time from Robert Frost, a simple, nearly insignificant line—*They leave us so to the way we took.* Bless her heart. Here, as it comes back to me, I mingle this into a dozen meanings, but all come out in the end applying to that railroad journey into the unknown. *They*, must mean my father, since he was the one who left. But for better or worse, *we*, in the end, decide who we will become and where we chose to take ourselves, burdens and all.

Only now, at sixty-five, and well-seasoned in many ways, I am able to look back into time at myself, as the twenty-six year old Sam Witt and see myself for what I was—an infant. A diapered crybaby of self-pity. I hadn't done enough in life yet to be self-important, but I continued to carry what I considered this identity everywhere, that of a fatherless orphan raised in a loveless world. It was too soon in my journey to realize that this bitter hate I carried had actually sprung from something else, like an underground spring, entirely mysterious and unknown to me.

It is the lesson everyone could benefit from learning, that even if we don't receive love from where we should, it doesn't mean it doesn't exist. If you can't find it by looking, then it will have to find you. And it usually does.

When North Dakota turned into Montana, the summer June sun was like a boil on the vast prairie, sending up gassy mirages in the far off reaches of a skillet-hot landscape. More cattle appeared on the soft sway of the hills where what seemed like wilderness, grass covered everything. And then finally there was the river.

"What's that?" I asked the women sitting across from me. She was gray-headed with a basket of knitting in her lap. Her glasses were on the point of her nose and when she looked up at me I saw her green eyes, stealing years from her etched face, making her look young. Eyes can do that. She looked out the window and tapped the glass with her knitting needle.

"Why, that's the Yellowstone. Isn't she a beaut?"

"Are you a native?"

She chuckled. "I am a Montanan, if that's what you mean. The Indians are the natives. They were here first." Her words were cool and patronizing.

I considered this an all-purpose answer, standard to the times, which even a clod from Cincinnati understood. Ohio had its own Indian stories. Many of them in fact. In junior high English class we were required to read *A Light in the Forest*, what would become a classic by Conrad Richter. *Old Yeller* too, and *Where the Red Fern Grows*, back when English teachers and history teachers were in cahoots, offering books that covered both subjects, killing two birds with one stone. After coming back from Eltopia, I would find myself delving deeply into Richter's other amazing books, *The Sea of Grass*, and his trilogy, *The Trees*, *The Fields*, and *The Town*.

"Isn't that where Custer met his doom? On the Yellowstone?"

This seemed to perturb the old woman. "Where have you been, young man? Please don't tell me you're from New York City."

"Cincinnati."

"Just as bad. Don't people in Cincinnati read?"

At this scolding I didn't dare confess that I taught history. She would have mocked me to a shameful death. Basically, she already had.

"River battles were everywhere back then. Yes, the Yellowstone. The Rosebud. The Bighorn and the Little Bighorn. This whole land belonged to Crazy Horse and Sitting Bull once. And Gall. They were once the prince-warriors. Until the government had better ideas. Or worse, depending on which side of history you're on."

I had been outdone by an old knitter with iron colored hair and glasses that moved on her nose when she talked.

"Riding through Montana isn't the same as setting foot on it. How far are you going? Seattle? God forbid."

"I am going to Washington, but not Seattle."

"You going there to stay or are you going back to Cincinnati?"

"My stay will be brief."

"Then let me give you some friendly advice, if I may. Take in Butte on the way back. Home of the copper kings and the big boom city on the hill. Then Bozeman, the north end of the Bozeman Trail which was what flustered old Red Cloud enough to start a war. Billings is a tough Cowtown. Always has been. And then there's Custer's Battlefield, as it's called. Was a pretty quick battle by battle standards. Crow Agency. Crows sided with the army to guide the troops." She laughed. "Guided Custer to his humiliation, they did." She paused, locking her green eyes on me. "But get your butt out of the seat and kick up some good Montana dust where all this stuff happened. You might learn a thing or two. Where do you work?"

I blinked. "A...hotel," I lied.

"That's nice. Well, my stop is coming up. It's been interesting visiting with you." She wound her ball of yarn and gathered her basket. She stood to straighten her long blue dress. "I passed through Cincinnati once," she said. "Too crowded."

I watched her leave down the aisle, hating her and loving her at the same time.

———

When I was in the third grade my teacher was Mr. Logan and he had a phonograph in his room. On certain days he would pull out an old black record, put it on the turntable, and *The Battle Hymn of the Republic* would blast out of the tinny speaker. Mr. Logan was tall and thin and the year he was my teacher he grew a beard, the same as Abraham Lincoln's. He'd found a stovepipe hat somewhere and so on Abraham Lincoln's birthday, in February, he put on a long, dark suit and told the class we were to address him as Mr. Lincoln for that day, not Mr. Logan. He played the battle hymn about ten times that day, and read from a book that gave us a glimpse of Honest Abe's sense of humor.

It's a sad thing when we forget to thank a good teacher. At the time, as kids, they seem like gods to us, frightening and unapproachable in a world of adults. If students only knew how much it can mean to a teacher to have former students return, just to say hello. Enough of those can be better than a paycheck. Just like the old woman with the knitting basket. I would think about her many times in the years following Eltopia, and yet I'd never even had the foresight, or the common decency, to ask her name.

But the train chugged on and I dozed. When I woke we were in the mountains—enormous mountains. At last, the Rockies. We were traveling close to Canada at the top of the Continental Divide. What we called mountains in Ohio were mere foothills to these monsters. Even in June there were some peaks that still had snow on top, like some distant cake icing. While I had dozed, a man had taken up the seat across from me, where the knitting lady had once sat. His face was hidden behind a copy of a Bismarck newspaper. *Gemini 4 Takes Flight in Two- Man Voyage to Circle the Earth.*

It was numbing, nearly dumbing news. Strange as it was, staring at the headline, I felt a ridiculous notion of kinship with the two astronauts—Ed White and James McDivitt—in that we were doing something of the same thing, exploring new worlds. White's and McDivitt's new world had been seen only by a few others, but my new world had been seen by many, from that breed of mountain men, like Jim Bridger and Jedidiah Smith, to explorers like Lewis and Clark. And of course, as the knitting lady had said, *the Indians were here first*. But knowing that as I slept on the train, for the last leg of this long and tiring journey, two men had been cast up into the blackness of the universe, making passes around this very planet. It struck me not as a sobering thought, rather a drunken thought, for it was simply too bizarre to fathom.

Would space travel someday overshadow all previous historical events? World War II was already being called the war to save the world. And WWI has been falsely tagged, the war to end all wars. What could surpass that? I left my seat with these staggering thoughts on my mind and weaved my way through several cars until I reached the dining car. I wasn't hungry, but I needed coffee. I would be arriving in Spokane in the morning, and after that, Eltopia. I wanted my wits on this last night to prepare my mind for what I might face. In the end I ordered a grilled cheese sandwich and potato salad and nursed my coffee through three cups. There had been a map posted behind a frame showing the train's route across America, and I had studied it several times. I found stops in Spokane and then Ritzville where I would transfer onto a different route, southeast to a place called Pasco. But where was Eltopia? It appeared on no map.

My mind was turning mawkish. Did Eltopia even exist? Had this all been some kind of dour joke, or misunderstanding. Rod Serling's television program had just aired its final season in 1964, but images of that odd black and white program ran through my head, thinking of some of his shows, where things that were there really weren't there at all. Was anything real? The coffee wasn't working. I wandered back to my seat—the newspaper man was gone—and I slumped down. The United States was big, much bigger than I had ever imaged, and this train ride had worn me down. I sat with glassy eyes turned inward, and somewhere, under the clicking of the tracks through the mountains, I slept out my exhaustion.

Over the years I've seen a dozen movies showing a man standing on a railway platform, his suit travel-worn, tie loosened and a look of perplexed vacancy on his face. Spencer Tracy didn't look perplexed in *Bad Day at Black Rock*, but the hilly, open surroundings of the rail stop in Ritzville, where I made my transfer, was almost as barren. It was a small town of once-ago promise. Over time, my impression would change. As a long shot, I asked the ticket master at the depot if he knew who Nancy McGrath was. The small man wore a tight collar and gray, bristly mustache and was stamping papers with a rubber stamp. He lifted his head slowly, the way only ancient people can do, ancient and thoughtful, because every question deserves an answer, and in order to answer means to consider the question. A pair of round-rimmed spectacles laid on his desk, and he picked these up but before putting them on, he examined them, perhaps to see if they were real.

He finally looked at me, with the jurisdiction of a chemist, or a surgeon, putting everything into the study of my face. He looked at me like this for a long time, as if trying to place me. Did he think I was a forgotten relative, or a movie star he'd seen a poster of? His gaze forced me to look away momentarily, at the street behind me, at the sky, at a raven hopping by the tracks, his prolonged examination unnerving me.

Finally he spoke. "Nancy McGrath? Of course I know her. She comes up here once a week. So long as there's mail."

I remembered then that Nancy McGrath had signed the telegram as *postmistress*.

The ticket master continued. "Nancy runs the little post office in Eltopia, same as her father did for thirty-two years. She collects the mail from the locals but has to bring it up here to put it on the train. For the out of county mail, that is. She brings local mail up here to our post office and collects anything addressed to Eltopia. It seems a bit outdated, but it works for us. Well, it works for her. It's not broken, so we haven't found a reason to fix it."

This speech took nearly five minutes to deliver, but through the whole time he kept that peculiar gaze on me. Finally, curious if he stared at everyone like this, I said, "Have you mistaken me for someone?"

He shook his head slowly. "Not mistaken. There couldn't be any mistaken."

"Mistaken?" I said. "About what?" Was this a puzzle of some sort? And if it was, was it unfolding, or getting tighter.

"If you're not Norman Witt's boy, I'll eat a cow pie."

I felt as if struck by a steel rod.

"A little late though, don't you think?" He said this scornfully.

Suddenly, as if on some divinely ordered que, the train's whistle let out a horrific scream, stiffening me and nearly forcing out my own scream. *A little late? What the hell was that supposed to mean?* I felt like grabbing the old man by the shirt collar and forcing his face into that cow pie.

"That's your train. And that's the last whistle." His own face had taken on a shadowy expression of judgment. He immediately removed his glasses and went back to his stamping, ignoring my glower of confused anger boring into the top of his head.

These are hard thoughts to remember. All these years later, the power of them remains, circling my study like a vibration, echoing in a way even the rain on the window cannot mollify. It was the first time I ever remember my father's name being spoken by anyone other than my vengeful mother, and he a total stranger, two thousand miles from home. It was both a shock and an insult. And as it turned out, a flash point to the next twenty-four hours.

It was as if I were on Gemini 4, arcing through an abysmal meteor storm, my head alive like a bomb. The fuse had been lit, and it would take a remaking of myself—in a sense, an explosion—before the life I had lived for twenty-six years would suffer both the loss and the gain of my waiting osmosis.

First impressions, they say, are critical. This last leg of my journey, from Ritzville to Eltopia was a study in geology where the land was at once desolate in its emptiness. Scab-rocked arroyos of basalt dropping into deeper ravines where yellow grass and brittle spreads of sagebrush populated the gaps and fields. Occasionally a square or triangle of green wheat covered a hillside with the odd workings of water being sprinkled from an irrigation system on wheels. Young corn too, the closer we got to our destination, and once, an actual lush valley where cattle grazed contentedly by a creek. But to me it still seemed like a vast and sparse wilderness.

As the train began to slow I could feel the pounding of blood in my ears. Did I have the courage to go through with this? My mother would be outraged, and though I believed I understood this outrage, I would learn in time, in the midst of an altogether worse rainstorm, the truer colors of many people, with a full measure of my own outrage. Out the window I saw what I fully expected to see, a smudge of a town on a hillside, little more than a hamlet, squared by small fences—were those sheep?—trailer houses mixed with clapboard houses, a small cafe on the front street, with a faulty neon sign that just said *CAF*, and two tall structures I would learn were for depositing and storing the wheat of nearby farmers. But the one building, an unusual shade of yellowish-tan, was a two story building with lettering on the fascia I could see clearly from the train, announcing Eltopia Schoolhouse. It was set on a hill. A block away a smaller building was tucked under a tree, a United States flag swirling from a pole.

In what seemed a mere passing of seconds, I gathered my suitcase and with scarcely a blink, found myself standing on a gravel path near a wooden post with a red reflector attached to it, apparently serving as Eltopia's official rail stop. The town was a quarter-mile further down the gravel lane, so I put my suitcase down and took another critical look at the place my father decided to claim as his home.

The train growled behind me, and with typical indifference picked up speed, as if peeved it had to stop in the first place, leaving me standing senseless in its slipstream. Off in the distance I heard the sheep bleating, and felt a kindred foolishness to their cries. In most every way, principally in the Bible, I would learn later, humans are associated with sheep, dumb and wandering as they are, and in desperate need of a shepherd. Here was my own version of a parable.

As the train disappeared further down the valley, a peculiar quietness settled around me. I felt bolted to the ground. It was a sensation I had felt before, on the very first day of my teaching career, staring at the wondering faces in my new classroom, knowing them only as strangers. I felt as if staring into a firing squad, convicted before even starting. Had the ticket man in Ritzville been an unwelcome warning of what might be awaiting me here. I longed for a sound, any sound. The sheep in the nearest pasture stood erect, looked at me as with a knowing pity. Finally a car passed behind me on the highway, shaking me out of my fearsome reverie.

In my apartment in Cincinnati, I would often wake on weekends to the sound of a piano, seeping through my window from another window across the alley. It was a young girl, living with her mother I learned, who would practice for an hour every Saturday morning. The girl's range was delicious, her ability beyond her years—I saw her from time to time through open curtains and judged her to be barely nine or ten. But she played as if her own heart rested on the keys, nothing brisk or unsophisticated, rather slow and thoughtful melodies that puts peace to the soul. Her name was Rosalee; I heard her mother call her once when the morning was still and noiseless. Now, walking slowly up the road into Eltopia, it was Rosalee's sweet renderings I longed to hear most.

But soon came the grumbling of trucks as they lined up in front of the wheat towers, waiting to dump their loads. I would learn later that it was loads of last year's wheat being transferred from farm silos to the railhead, it being too early for this year's harvest. But it created a constant billowing cloud of chaff to hang over the wide warehouse doors. And inside this swirling veil I could see the ghostly form of a man, motioning for the next truck to enter and dump. I stopped for a moment, staring at the man, whose arms seemed always in motion. As each truck pulled forward over a grate, the man pulled a lever on the back of the truck and wheat spilled out like a slender waterfall. Rosalee's music ceased playing in my head.

I sized-up the cafe as I drew near. An old man in coveralls was sitting on a bench out front, fiddling at something with knobby fingers. Closer, I saw he was filling his pipe with tobacco, tamping it down with his thumb. He produced a flame, touched it to the bowl and puffed, and then he looked up at me. His first reaction was one of confused recognition, a slight start, and then, as apparent realization set in, he offered me a scowl and turned away. *Again*, I thought. It was the second time I was being judged by what, I assumed was my appearance. The ticket man in Ritzville recognized me without effort for being a

Witt. Had this old man done the same thing, or was he simply Eltopia's unwelcome committee.

I ignored him and pushed open the cafe door.

It is never easy to take in the finer details of an entire room upon first entering, and even as small as this cafe was, it was a challenge to focus. I was the proverbial *new-man-in-town*, in a town where there were never new-men, and I looked every bit the part, suitcase in hand, brow-knitting look of bewilderment on my face. There were stools at the counter, and three booths snugged against the facing windows. A jukebox in the corner was pouring out some country song, about someone having fought the law, but the law won. Around the corner, in the rear, where the room formed an L-shape, I heard the unmistakable clacking of pool balls being hit. I absorbed all of this within the passing of fifteen seconds.

A man sitting at the counter swiveled in his stool and looked at me. He was stout, about fifty or so years old, dressed in farmer's garb, and a salt and pepper mustache. Upon seeing me, his hand went to his chin as if stroking a beard that wasn't there. His eyes were deep set and contemplative. He pursed his lips then and turned back to his supper. Then, beyond him, and through the opening into the kitchen, I caught the staring eyes of the cook. His forehead and chin were in shadow, but his piercing eyes were in a bright swath of light, like that of a forest animal, all penetrating as if peering out from his den. I saw his mouth move, and within an instant he was joined by the face of a young woman.

Still holding my suitcase, I turned and followed the sound of the pool game. These two were younger men, closer to my age, but also in the wardrobe of farmers. One wore a cowboy hat, battered into comfort, and the other a sweat-banded ball cap. Two bottles of beer rested on the table skirt and a girl, sitting on a stool in the shadows, was smoking a cigarette. She was pretty but hard, her pant legs tucked into a pair of high cowboy boots. She smiled at me, then called to one of the pool players—"Kevin."

Kevin finished his shot then turned. Seeing me his eyes widened noticeably, but did not carry the customary hostility I'd been getting.

He nodded offhandedly then returned to his game. By then the girl had risen from her perch and came straight to me. "If you ain't a hell of a sight."

"Excuse me," I said.

"The whole town's been wondering if you'd have the nerve to show up."

I shook my head dumbly. Words failed me, too many in my head, but none to reach my mouth. Finally, "Is...is it that obvious?"

"My name is Tami," she said and stuck out her hand. "And I don't have a horse in this race."

"What race?" I said, taking her hand, hesitantly.

"Whether you would show up or not. And I'll be honest, half the town was hoping you wouldn't."

I felt my shoulders sag. "Then...who does the town think I am?"

Tami smiled broadly. "If you're not Norman Witt's kid, then I'll join a monastery."

The pool game went on around us. I figured Tami was the property of Kevin, or the other way around. Either way, in spite of the overall awkwardness of the moment, she was the first friendly face I'd seen. Kevin glanced over at us occasionally with mixed interest, then went back to his game.

"So why the interest. In me?"

"Can I buy you a beer? You look train-weary."

I looked at her, trying to read through her prettiness for a sign of malice or trickery, but saw only a confident girl of few hang-ups. "Not now. Thanks. Maybe another time." I looked over at Kevin and noticed his partner, the cowboy hat guy, smiling with amusement at something; probably me.

Tami shrugged.

"Okay. I am Sam Witt. But that's as far as I'll go to claiming anything of Norman Witt's."

She stared past me for a moment, taking in the other customers. "There's lots of old men in this town, Sam Witt. They go back to the dam building years. They worked shoulder to shoulder with your...with Norman. To a good many of us, Norman Witt was a saint."

"He was a son of a bitch."

She did not flinch from my words. Instead, she said, "There's always that other side."

"I only know one side. Mine."

"That's not likely to surprise anyone here. Some of these old timers expected you to come here fifteen years ago. Back when you were just a kid. That's what Norman wanted. When you didn't, they set their minds against you."

"I...I would have been eleven."

"A good time for a son to be with his father. At least that was the talk."

My anger was rising but I didn't want it directed at the only civil person I'd met so far. "Look. I'd like to know how to find Nancy McGrath."

Tami smiled again. "That'll be easy." She tilted her head. "Up the hill. Follow the flagpole. She mans the post office. If she's not there, her house is the gray one set back in the trees. Can't miss it." She said all this with a curl to her lips, as if some form of private humor lay there. "Knowing Nancy, she's probably still at the post office. Behind her cage." Now her smile was full.

"Am I missing something?"

"No, Sam. It just might be best to find Nancy before the locals arrive for their chow. By now they probably all know you're here. They might need a time to digest that information."

I looked at Tami. "Is this a case of the spider and the fly?"

"With me?" she said. "Not me. I'm not the spider. I'm a neutral. One of the rare ones."

"Okay. That's better than I've been getting. I appreciate it, Tami."

As I returned to the dining area, the young woman who'd stared at me from through the cook's portal came to me. She was in a pink waitress dress with an apron and name badge, announcing her as Oline.

"You're leaving? Didn't you want something to eat? "Her chestnut hair was shoulder length and her blue eyes seemed sincere.

I shook my head. I had lost both my appetite and my civility. I brushed by her and left through the front door. The pipe smoker was still there, offering up only a grunt of disapproval.

It is my wife who delves into the poetics. My interests have always lain in the less abstract, of connecting the past with the today of our lives, of the uncovered bones, as it was so long ago when I grieved for Tatiana Romanov, of the unnecessary and violent death of her youthful life. That was then. But since, my wife has taught me that it is often the poets who have recorded history best. *And who better*, she said, *than Walt Whitman*. And, as wives usually are, she was right. And so now, as I remember trekking up this dirt road towards the Eltopia post office, it is, looking back, the opening and closing lines of a Whitman poem that should have lodged in my head that day—*In paths untrodden...to tell the secret of my nights and days...*

The sun was making its westward slant, burning a dusky red over the hills and behind the trees. I continued to be the subject of the sheep, whose woolly, curious black faces watched my every step. I tried to think of omens, but if this was one, I reached the flagpole quickly and stopped to look around. Apparently I had made my escape just in time, as below several pickup trucks and emptied wheat trucks were just then stopping in front of the cafe. I watched as men, young and old piled out and headed inside. Further on I could see the warehouse and the elevators. The lean man I'd seen earlier was still standing there, and whether it was real or just my imagination, it looked as if he was staring up at me, a lone figure on the hill.

A light was burning in the post office, so I turned and headed for the door. I stopped one last time and looked back. The man was still there, head tilted up, as if eyeing my every move. I turned and entered the post office, barely the size of a living room. And just as Tami had said, there was a cage, separating the back room from the front, and the rented mailboxes and counter. I heard a bustle behind the cage and waited. Setting down my suitcase, I gave a hello. *Just a minute*, was the reply.

Sight unseen is a dangerous thing, especially when buying, say, a sofa, or a used car. No one really does that. So, standing there—for more than a minute—I imagined a woman in her mid-sixties with graying hair and out of fashioned spectacles. But the Nancy McGrath that finally emerged from the back room was nothing of the kind. Blonde hair, dark eyes, full lips with a delicate smear of red lipstick, and a flowered blouse open at the front, just enough to show fine, tanned skin. I judged her to be in her late thirties or early forties.

But I was not the only one taking inventory. Even from behind her cage I could see her eyes widen. Her mouth opened part way but no words came out. Not immediately. When she finally did speak it was barely a whisper. "You are Sam Witt, aren't you?" Her eyes continued taking me in. "Of course you are. My God, you are the spitting image of your father."

I had already begun realizing this, but here was a straight up declaration. Because of my loathing of my father, this was not pleasing news. Was this resemblance some form of revenge, like a family scar passed on? Nancy McGrath came hurriedly around from behind the cage and taking my hand began pumping. "You didn't reply to my telegram, so I really had no idea if you'd be coming."

Standing this close to her I was taken by the surprise of her casual good looks. I rather forgot about my father for the moment and stood dumbly before her.

"You've come at a good time," she said, then touched my arm familiarly, as if forgetting I was Sam and not Norman. As she examined me I believe I saw her face color.

"I've prepared the little cabin out back in the hopes you'd come. It's where your father stayed."

Frowning, I said, "I'd prefer a motel."

Nancy McGrath stifled a laugh. "No such things as motels here, I'm afraid. It's my little cabin or...or the stars." She took me by the sleeve. "I can show you now. I'm done here anyway. Take up your suitcase and we'll go."

Clearly, there was no room to argue. I followed her from the post office a mere half block to where the gray house Tami had spoken of rested, surrounded by a cluster of tall elms. The house itself was constructed simply of shiplap with green shuttered windows. The shutters were open and the window glass was reflecting the red sinking sun. There was a lawn, unmown but green, and as we passed the house into the deeper part of the yard, I saw what apparently was the cabin. It was small, with two curtained windows and a windowed brown door.

Nancy McGrath was wearing blue jeans, and as she walked before me I noticed the pleasing curvature of her backside. She was trim and well-proportioned and it lent itself to her power of persuasion, that of insisting I stay in the cabin. She was older than me by ten or twelve years, but that alone added to the persuasion. For a moment I almost wished Mercedes had come with me so that I'd have someone to share this place with, and relieve some of the anxiety growing inside me.

As she fumbled for the key—it was locked, she said, to protect my father's belongings from busybodies—I glanced further into the darkening yard and saw another, much smaller shed, hidden behind an overhanging crabapple tree. It set itself apart from the rest of the yard, both in direction and in an odd allure. When we dream of houses, it's been said, the house is actually a representation of the dreamer, of oneself. But here, this little shed was like a creature unto itself. Ill-kept, it was, with a cluster of vines encircling it, and had it eyes, they would have stared with reproach from the shadows.

Nancy McGrath swung open the cabin door and then turned to me. She saw that I was looking at the little shed and waved her hand dismissively. "Never mind that. It's the pump house. If you hear humming coming from there, it's only the pump churning out water." She beckoned me inside the cabin with a nod, then flipping on a light switch the little single room lit up. It was primitive, with dull, colorless wallpaper, a single bunk against one wall, a small writer's desk, a closet the size of a phone booth, and a single bookshelf. Alongside the desk was a sea chest, secured with a padlock. As if following my eyes and my thoughts, *Nancy* McGrath reached inside her jacket pocket and produced a key.

"Because your father lived here these past years, I felt it my responsibility to keep his belongings in the chest." She said this while holding the key out to me. "I washed all the bedding. In the event you might show up. Everything is fresh."

I wasn't interested in my father's belongings, but I took the key, more as an act of obedience. A myriad of different feelings were flooding my mind at that moment—the very absurdity of me being here in the first place; the unexpected attractiveness of Nancy McGrath; but mostly the surreal realization that I had finally tracked down the man I despised, only to find out that the glamorous life I imaged him having was reduced to a one room cabin, with nary a telltale sign of personal eminence. My mind was a muddle.

"Of course, Norman kept to himself. Generally." Saying this, she stepped back out of the cabin, standing in the ruby light of the gloaming. It radiated in her hair, putting a more brilliant quality to her face. She turned and smiled at me. "I will be warming up some supper in a bit. Nothing special. But I would find your company welcome. Provided you don't mind. I'm open to answering any questions you might have about your father."

I watched her walk across the lawn to her back door, open it and go inside.

For the next thirty minutes I simply sat on the bunk and stared at the sea chest. How far I was from all things familiar to me. What, I wondered, was Mercedes doing at that very moment? Without thinking, I didn't even know what day it was. Was little Rosalee at her piano? Was Ashley getting ready for bed? Or was she sitting naked in a bathtub full of bubbles. It was two hours later in Cincinnati now. Or was it three hours. Who knew? I was lost. What the hell had I been thinking, to come out here?

Routine was my forte. The realization to this had come slowly, but by the time I had taught school for a year, it dawned on me that I was a creature of well-developed habit. In my little apartment kitchen, the salt and pepper shakers had their place, and rarely were found outside of that. My chair at the small table was always pushed in after eating. My clothes were hung up neatly after being laundered, which was

Thursdays after work, religiously. My two pair of shoes had their place beside the closet door; my bedroom window was open two inches in the winter and halfway up in the summer; dishes were washed after every meal, dried and put away. It wasn't that I was some kind of perfectionist freak, it was just the way things had developed, and if I wanted them done, I had to do them myself.

Mercedes had been a major disruption to all this, and she, being a clever cat, purposely did things to mess with my routine. Sometimes she was sly about it, and other times she did it as an act of open defiance, hoping to start either a discussion, or a full blown argument, it didn't matter which. And here I was again, sitting in this little cabin in Eltopia, a peculiar little hamlet, so out of my routine, it was almost like having an ulcer, or severe heartburn. One minute I was exhausted, and the next, I wasn't. Nancy McGrath finally called me in from the back door, and so, with equal measures of resentment and curiosity, I ventured across the lawn and into an evening of bewildered enlightenment, what my wife would once call *the teeter-totter of balance*, between truth and fiction.

The hallway through which she led me toward the kitchen was dim, and every adjoining room branching off from there was clothed in darkness, as if her message was: *Here is the light at the end of the tunnel, follow me.* Which I did. And here, in yellow light, was a typical kitchen equipped with sink and counter top, a four-burner stove, refrigerator, a pantry with the door partially open, and in the center stood a small Formica table on chrome legs, with two matching orange-cushioned chairs, also with chrome legs. She had put a vase of flowers in the center of the table, a new addition, perhaps for the occasion, because I noticed several fresh drops of water that had dripped on the tabletop.

"Leftover pork roast from last night. I don't get many dinner guests. But the potatoes are fresh, but the peas are from a can." She pointed to a mixing bowl on the counter. "I'm working on some cookie dough for later."

I sat stupidly, watching her. She had changed into a pair of tan pants that, like her jeans fit nicely around her ass, which was hard to ignore when her back was turned. A flowered, long-sleeved blouse had replaced her postal jacket and it seemed as if she had freshened her lipstick.

"I can offer you coffee. Or would you rather have a beer? I don't drink beer but I always have a few on hand"

I was not thinking of coffee or beer, but because of my hesitation, she decided for me, placing a bottle of Rainier in front of me. "It was..." She seemed to catch herself suddenly and feigned absentmindedness by turning back to the cupboard and fetching two plates. "I fear I am an awkward hostess."

As she set the table I noticed a slight tremor to her hands which hadn't been there before. Was my presence really something she had expected? Was she nervous? She rather seemed it. But why? I was the one who should be feeling uncomfortable, considering the circumstances. And then it came to me, like a blow alongside the head. It was my father, Norman Witt who would normally be sitting in my place. And her unfinished sentence—*It was...* It was the beer. The Rainier. It was his favorite beer, that's what she almost said. My mind swam. Had this woman and my father been...lovers?

She had placed the food before us and had sat down across from me, yet I hadn't even noticed, I was busy staring at the beer bottle. The absurdity of the mind while under stress. I foolishly remembered being chased from a downtown park once when I was young by a swarm of bees, who just happened to be building a hive in a tree. I remember running, waving my hands over my head. Sitting here, my explosion of thoughts was like those bees, and I wondered if jumping up and waving my arms might put an end to this whole crazy affair.

I looked across the table at Nancy McGrath and was suddenly seized with an odd kind of envy. Or was it simple jealousy. Had my father made love to this plain, yet attractive woman? *The bastard*, I thought. And yet, aside from my hatred, I tried comparing this attractive woman to the shrew my mother had become, and found myself not blaming him. But! Was I sitting in his chair now? I was about to be drinking his beer. His Rainier. And unless I decided to sleep with the sheep in their pasture, I would be in the same bed that Norman Witt had slept in; dreamt in; and—

"You're not eating. Is my fare too ordinary?"

Startled, I found my voice. "No...no, really. I am a notoriously low class eater. This looks like a feast compared to my Chinese take-out. Or my TV dinners. I'm a simple man." I quickly filled my mouth with mashed potatoes to shut off my foolish words.

And so began the fulfillment of what this visit, and especially this meal was to represent—an uncovering and revealing of information, about who Norman Witt was, and who Sam Witt is. Nancy McGrath was nothing if not tactful. She knew how to broach a subject, but once opened, how to ask all the right questions. Her interest seemed honest, and her tact gentle. If this woman was my father's lover, than what could I possibly lose by lying. She probably already knew most of the answers already. From Norman's side of the story anyway. He wasn't here to dispute my version. By the time the meal was finished, I had told her about my life to that point and how I owed no thanks to my father for whatever I had achieved. I even confessed, probably for shock value, my escapades with Mercedes. Would this woman's fantasies, if she had any, include bedding the son of her former lover? Women, in general, remained that much of a mystery to me that I could only wonder. Or was it my own fantasy.

She finally did make some coffee, and then, after washing her hands, began kneading her cookie dough, talking over her shoulder. At one point she said, "I imagine your hands are stronger than mine. I may have added too much flour. Would you please? Wash your hands in the sink here and give this dough a good workout while I find the chocolate chips"

It did not come across as a request. And as ridiculous as it felt, putting my hands in a bowl of cookie dough, in the kitchen of an utter stranger, I found myself obeying. Of course, watching my hands and fingers squeezing the cream colored dough, it became the essence of other things. So, in order to distract myself, I asked her about the man at the warehouse, the one who had watched me climb the hill to the post office.

Nancy McGrath had found the chocolate chips and stood before me with the open bag. My question caused her to stiffen slightly. "Oh, him.

That is Reuben Flett. He's an Indian and it would be my advice you stay clear of him. He's trouble."

There was no reason to doubt her, as his behavior towards me had already been unsettling. But I forged ahead. "What kind of trouble?"

She poured in nearly the whole bag of chocolate chips, and then, because the bowl was big, she plunged her hands inside alongside mine. I wondered for a moment if it wasn't to steady her hands from shaking. But regardless, as our fingers occasionally became intertwined, it took on a bizarre form of intimacy. Before answering she playfully grabbed for one of my fingers and then smiled hard into my open face.

"Trouble? Oh, Reuben Flett claimed a friendship with your father that...that I doubted was genuine. Not honest, in other words."

"How old is he?"

Her shoulders sagged, as if ready for this questioning to be over. "Oh, I don't know. Around your age, I suppose. How old are you?" She lifted her eyes and made to study me.

"Twenty-six," I said.

That penetrating smile again.

I waited.

"Reuben's probably twenty-eight or nine." Then, quickly, "Here, give me your hands and I'll get the dough off of you. Then you can wash up again." She took each of my fingers in her hands and pulled on them, as if drawing me closer into her curious level of sentiment. There was no question now that I had stumbled into some kind of oddity. It was beginning to remind me of how Mercedes had maneuvered events to snare me into her clutches. I felt a rush of discomfort. Nancy McGrath was behaving in an unnaturally familiar way for having known me barely two hours. And yet, she had known my father. Was that who she was seeing tonight? How much cookie dough had my father kneaded? And what else had his hands kneaded? And then, suddenly, Nancy McGrath began talking again.

"Reuben Flett lives in a dumpy trailer house over the hill. With a corral full of horses and a nasty dog. His folks were run off their place when they put the dam in. It was a sad story, if it's even true, and I think your father's soft heart got the best of him." She put a dozen blobs of dough on a cookie sheet and put it in the oven.

For a man she supposedly disliked, she was talking a lot about him. I sipped my coffee and listened, watching the curve of her elbow and the gentle swish of her wrist as she prepared a second cookie sheet with dough. A curl of blonde hair had fallen over her ear and I noticed for the first time that she was wearing a pretty pair of earrings. Her hands were steady now, no more mild shaking, and once, reaching up to push away her hair, her shirt rose up to expose a three-inch patch of skin at her waist. It was not tan, like her arms, rather the unexposed rosy blush of a powder puff, the sight of it titillating.

For another half hour we ate cookies and drank coffee and the subject of either Reuben Flett or my father never came back up, only light talk about the mail that she would drive up to Ritzville in the morning and the hope of rain in the not too far off. The kitchen seemed to shrink around us and for a time I could almost imagine that time in this crazy little town might not even exist. There were moments when the level of comfort rose, and the sound of her voice such a welcome, that I dreaded ever leaving to go back to the cabin. But I thanked her and stood to go. She put a half dozen cookies on a paper plate for me to take with me and then walked me to the door. She turned on a yard light and pointed me to the cabin where an odd and unwelcome darkness seemed to wash through the trees.

Down the hall from my study I can hear my wife stir. Our plane to Spokane is hours away from leaving, and since we packed last night, there is no reason to rush. The taxi ride will take less than twenty minutes. Eventually we'll shower and then sit in the nook and drink our customary coffee. We'll speak of Reuben in wordless eye-talk, and smile at each other in the secret way our love works. Normally I would be checking the box scores to see if the Reds had any luck last night, but not this morning. Then again, perhaps I should. It was Reuben's habit that became my own.

Here is my morning for contemplation. My wife took me to a

production of Tennessee William's *The Glass Menagerie* some years back. It was a good play, albeit unsettling in its lonely air. But she has taught me how to remember significant lines of literature that might have relevance someday. Here is that day. I forget which of Williams's characters said it, but it sits staring back at me through this rainy window—*Time is the longest distance between two places.*

Eltopia is the obvious place, of course. But it goes beyond that. To Normandy. To Market Garden and then the Battle of the Bulge. And finally to the liberation of Kaufering. Places where my father fought. I dream sometimes, as I did early this very morning, that he and I are sitting in a foxhole together, the sharp edges of our differing lives sparking like flints. How very far time takes us without a word of preparation. Without a word of apology. Young people—the very young people I teach—have a faulty view of time, as if they own it somehow. But time is the one thing that shows no pity for those who misuse it. It stares at you every day from the mirror, defying your defective wisdom. Time ends up outsmarting us all.

Sleeping in my father's bed in Nancy McGrath's cabin was like sleeping on a bed of nails. In the many ways that history unfolds itself, I wrestled through the night as if an archeologist who accidently stumbled onto some strange, fertile soil. If ever I was to understand anything about who my father was, or even who I was, it would have to start here, digging up old bones. But my self-pitying rage was too strong.

I stared at the sea chest in the corner with the repulsion of a leper. It was a Pandora's Box I wanted no part of. But in trying to dissect the several hours I had just spent with Nancy McGrath, I found myself looking at a poorly drawn map, with crooked roads leading in a thousand different directions. How had she so easily drawn me into something as irrational as putting my hands in a bowl of cookie dough? Even in the darkness of the cabin I could feel my face color in shame. The spider and the fly? Tami, down at the pool table, had said, *Not me. I'm not the spider.* But she didn't deny that there might be a spider. That left Nancy McGrath. I had caught Tami's ever so slight grin of condescendence at the post mistress's name.

Finally figuring out that it was Tuesday, almost Wednesday, as midnight approached, I remembered the telegraph informing me that the train ran Tuesdays and Fridays. That left me stranded in Eltopia for a couple more days. But hadn't Nancy McGrath said she had to take mail to Ritzville in the morning? Maybe I could get a ride with her, catch a train from there and exit this place. It was feeling more and more like a huge mistake, being here. My father was dead and good riddance. He died in my life years ago. Sticking it out with Mercedes Belfour might have been the better of two hells.

Still, there was something unsettling about Nancy McGrath, about the way she had so effortlessly pulled me into her maneuvering. Was it her stealth, or my own artless mishandling of myself? But I also remembered the uneasiness I felt when I wasn't sure if it was me, or my dead father, who she saw sitting at her table. And her sometimes shaking hands, faint but noticeable, that only seemed to come when the mention of Norman Witt came up. Or was it something totally unrelated, like the onset of Parkinson's? Not likely. She seemed the picture of country health. And what if they had been lovers, my father and she? Was that any less or great a crime than walking away from his family?

The window beckoned me and so I rose from bed and stood staring up at the circle of moon. From there I could see the dark outline of the house, the windows oddly vacant of light, with only the shadow of the eaves and gable edges to add contrast to the thick, even darker trees. It was June and the heat had scarcely receded from the warm day. The cabin was stuffy, so I opened the door and stepped out onto the lawn. I imagined for a moment my father doing this very thing. Stepping outside to get some fresh air against the stillness of the cabin. Or, I wondered, would he be sleeping in the house, alongside a naked Nancy McGrath.

I stared at stars I had no names for, only realizing they were oddly the same stars I could see from Cincinnati, at those rare moments when I took the time to look up. But here, in this dark yard, they were thick as a carpet, and layered into a depth of universe I'd never seen before. Here was a complexity to match my own situation, an expanse so vast that reaching any conclusions seemed pointless. But as I turned to go back in the cabin I saw the silhouette of the little shed, set deep into the dark yard. The pump house, she'd called it. It released a foreboding presence, as if alive, and I found myself shying away from it.

———

I am proud of my wife's curiosity when it comes to literature, and her then ability to transform the message of it into her classroom curriculum, leaving me with the table crumbs that gather at my feet. Her excitement and enthusiasm over new things, and her willingness to share them with me, has, after so many years, made me a joint beneficiary. Though Scottish poet, Joseph Lee, has lost some of his ranking as a World War I poet, in the shadow of Wilfred Owen, Siegfried Sassoon, and Rupert Brookes, Lee's work caught my wife's eye some years back. At the time, it was noted by her for its cultural importance and use of old English. But now, with the passing of Reuben on my mind, a gathering of lines from his poem, *The Gate of Departure*, seems more than fitting.

I mouth them now to myself—*O' sun and shade, and wind and rain / O, night and day—and death amain / And times that shall not be again.*

And it is a cavalcade of other faces too, not just Reuben Flett's. There is Ashley Given's face, she who never married and just recently retired from the bank where she gave almost the entirety of her working life. Her retirement was posted in the newspaper, her photograph showing a youthful sixty-two years old. No matter how happily married a person can be, there seems that natural quality that wonders about alternative history. One's personal history. She was my first love, and so it is normal that I wonder what our lives might have been like had we continued our romance. But such things are only for daydreamers. Things were as they must have been meant to be.

Mercedes Belfour, it turns out, married several times, each time for money, though she had plenty of her own. When she learned I was to be married, she came to me one last time, with the bold question— *Does this mean there's no more chance for us?* By that time I could only be gentle, seeing her in the new light of so many changes in my life. I won't say it was pity, for I was wrestling at that time with my own self-pity, but it was something close to it, for I felt I could see the road she was about to venture down—which she did, eventually—and I did not envy her that. She kept her beauty through her forties, but I saw her once, from a distance, and the energy and fight that was once her trademark, seemed to have gone out of her. Too many husbands can do that, I suppose. *And times that shall not be again.* No, it was a season of confused lust, which for me, was thankfully replaced by love.

Outside the cabin I heard the sound of a car being revved. I blinked awake, forgetting altogether where I was. It was early but being June, the sun had been long up. It took me another minute to realize that the sound was Nancy McGrath's car and she was going to Ritzville. I leapt from the bed and parted the curtain on the door just in time to see her blue station wagon turn out of the yard and head down the hill for the highway.

I had slept through my only chance for escape. Returning to the bed I punched the pillow in disgust. It was Wednesday and I would now be a prisoner until Friday. The only thing remotely resembling a blessing was the tiny shower stall in the back corner of the cabin, with its miniature sink and toilet. But I didn't even have a book to read. Or a newspaper. I had read fantastical stories when I was younger about time warps, where people slipped into another realm, and forced to live out their days roaming the hay fields and milk barns of ancient villages in Europe. I had, at one point, stopped reading H. P. Lovecraft for the very horror he put on my nights. Eltopia was so like that I feared giving it too much energy, lest it come true.

Considering my options, I showered, dressed and set out, deciding to have breakfast at the diner in the hope that the civility had taken a turn for the better. But emerging from Nancy McGrath's tree-gloomed yard, I immediately saw plainly what I had only vaguely seen the night before, and that was the big, oddly yellow two-story schoolhouse.

Having been a school teacher for three years now, I felt a peculiar kinship to schools. Right or wrong, I saw them as a haven of sorts. It was certainly the case at P.S. 17. In that rough neighborhood, where home life was often a mere step away from the turmoil of the street. It didn't always work out that way, but most teachers tried to give kids a place to escape too. Sadly, neighborhood troubles followed the kids to school. But the hope, at least, remained.

So I found myself wandering across a field of weeds to the open doors of the school. Outside, with the tailgate down was an old model pickup truck with a load of lumber on it. And as I drew closer I heard the sound of a circular saw biting into a chunk of wood. These were familiar sounds from P. S. 17's shop class on the bottom floor where Mr. Fracton—his students called him Mr. Fraction—tried to teach kids how to use tools without cutting off their fingers. Sometimes it worked.

But, since school was out here in Eltopia too, this was no shop class razing the morning peace. I stood for a while admiring the old building, its windows, its false Gothic corners and unusual whitewashed yellow paint. The grass of the playground was patchy with several galvanized crossbars and teeter-totters. Further back though, behind a wooden fence I saw a backstop of cyclone wire rising above a set of bleachers. I strolled to the wooden fence, which I now realized was the outfield home run fence, and looked over it. Here the grass was lush and green, the raised pitcher's mound scraped clean of weeds and the base paths trimmed neatly. The bleachers were old and wooden, but well-supported with fresh planking.

I had grown up following the Cincinnati Reds, America's oldest team, and when I could pickle-away enough loose change, I would head down to the stadium and buy a ticket for the cheap seats. There was never a television in Marion Witt's hovel so watching them had to be done either at a friend's house, both being rare, or to wander around the TV department of the Sears and Roebuck store, until a clerk would figure things out and run me off. Mostly though, it was the radio, and even now I preferred listening to them than watching them. Unless it was in person at the stadium.

I could smell sawdust coming from whatever was being done inside the school, so I ventured closer to the open front doors. I peered down the hallway, where a few desks and chairs were stacked out of the way, and a door opened further along, where I assumed the circular saw was at work. A peculiar strangeness surrounded me, as if I was entering a time tunnel. Schools were familiar to me, but this was different, as I entered further. I already felt a trespasser in this town, so the last thing I wanted was to be discovered snooping around.

There had been that pickup parked nearby with the lumber on it, so I figured as long as I heard the saw grinding away, whoever the worker was, he would not hear me. I walked carefully, looking around. To my right I detected the gleam of glass, and approaching I could see through its dimness that it was an award display, with an array of football, basketball and baseball trophies dating back years. There were pennants and team photographs, bronze cups and etched silver plates commemorating championship teams.

I moved on, closer to the open door. I was determined now to look into a classroom, even if it meant being discovered. I had no reason to be afraid of these people, since they didn't like me anyway I had nothing to lose. I had already missed my chance for escape when Nancy McGrath drove down the road to Ritzville.

As I drew closer to the open door, the scent of sawdust grew stronger and it was pleasant and reminded me of when I made occasional deliveries to Hillerman Lumber Yard when I worked for the auto parts store. I always wondered what it would be like to build something with my own two hands, but maybe some carpenters wondered what it would be like to stand in front of thirty-five kids and teach them something. On second thought, I doubted it. Like a few other things, I imagined carpentry was formed in a person's blood from birth.

Looking inside the room I saw the backside of a small man in overalls, turning a piece of plywood in his hands to size it up. It obviously had been cut to size, and would have a place to go. He heard my step and turned, and suddenly took a step back, in shock, or so it seemed.

"Damn you, kid. You gave me a start." He said this, all the while staring into my face.

"I'm sorry. I should have announced myself."

The man took off his cap and wiped his brow with his shirt sleeve. "It's not that. It's just...why, hell, we just lost your pa last week and now here you stand, a damn spittin' image. It just startled me."

He spoke these words without hostility.

"I've been getting a lot of that," I said, trying to keep an even tone.

"Well, I don't doubt that. Have you looked in a mirror lately?"

"That wouldn't do much good. I was five or six last time I saw him."

"So I heard."

"What did you hear?"

"Look, son. I thought the world of your pa. And whatever feelings you might have against or for him, I am not here to judge."

I held my tongue. My own words of hatred were getting tiresome even for me to hear.

The man was still holding the piece of plywood, and when he realized it, he quickly set it aside and dusting his hands together, stepped forward. "Names Shim. Shim Harden. I'm the school custodian here." He put out his hand.

Here was the complete reversal of anything I had seen, with the possible exception of Tami, and Nancy McGrath. I hesitated and then shook his hand. "Sam Witt, which I guess you already know."

"There's a lot of people in this town that think they got things figured out. Most of them are a pain in the ass. It ain't just you, son. They would judge the Virgin Mary if she showed up in a pickup instead of a donkey. Busy bodies is what they are."

I wondered what my next words should be and felt unsure of where I might tread, but I did have a few questions and maybe Shim Harden was the man to ask. "I'm staying in that little cabin that my father was living in. At Nancy McGrath's."

Shim was listening attentively.

"Since it appears I'll be stuck...well, unable to leave until Friday, I guess it might be prudent for me to stay clear of some people. The ones who so far have killed me with their stares."

"Ahh, there's those. Let 'em stare. Way I see it, everybody's got a story. I know your pa had his. But not once did he ever say a word against you. He tried hard to imagine some things, but in his own deepest thoughts, I reckon he had some answers."

Shim was getting more relaxed. He sat down on his sawhorses and motioned towards his thermos. "I can find a second cup if you're up for some coffee."

I shook my head. "Thanks, Mr. Harden. I was heading down to the cafe for some breakfast when I stopped here." I looked around the room, saw desks pushed out of the way, but I could still imagine a classroom full of kids in here, likely not much different than kids anywhere.

Sitting in my study now, the very picture of Shim Harden is illuminated in my mind, unforgettable in his hospitality and kindness. He was the first friend I had found in Eltopia, but not the last. In my mind's eye, I often give Shim a halo. True, there was sunlight coming through those classroom windows, and yes, if he stood in the proper place, a back-beam of that sunlight seemed at times to surround his head. But the halo was something he earned all on his own, for his sympathy and thoughtful nature.

"I've been told to stay clear of Reuben Flett. Is that sound advice?"

Shim pondered this for a long time. "I'm wondering who might have said that, but I think I know. Truth is, I doubt you'll be able to leave this town without seeing him. He'll pick his time."

"Is he trouble?"

Tilting his head to the side, Shim pondered again. "This can't be an easy thing to tell the son of Norman Witt. But truth is, your pa was like a father to Reuben. That boy, being a displaced Indian, was wild and angry as a wounded coyote. He came here to Eltopia almost by accident. Long story. He was about nine or ten, I guess. Today, Reuben is one of the hardest working young men in this town. It took a special man to tame that kid, but that's exactly what your pa did."

Shim Harden was right; they were hard words for me to hear. I had been replaced by an orphan Indian kid. If Norman Witt had taken such pains with an orphan, than why hadn't he collected his own orphan and tamed me?

"So," Shim went on, "there was nobody in this town hurt more than

Reuben when your pa died. He's still confused about the whole thing, and the towns a bit on edge about whether his anger will return. Seeing you, I mean."

I suddenly realized I hadn't even asked, much less wondered, how my father had died. Shim Harden seemed the person to ask. "What happened? How'd he die?"

As if struck himself by a deep sadness, Shim swiped at his nose, then tilted his head in the direction of the wheat elevators. "He fell. Up on the top level, doing something. He was working up there, and next thing anyone knows, he fell down past the elevator shaft and was killed. Fifty foot fall. No chance."

I was instantly sobered. In my mind, from the moment I read the telegram in my classroom to the long and wearisome train ride, I had never once considered how he might have died. One just takes for granted that he was sick. That he had a heart attack, or cancer. But this was stunningly different. Was it an accident? Or was it suicide?

"Where was Reuben Flett when this happened?"

"He got a call that his horses had knocked down the fence out at his place. So he was out tryin' to round 'em up before they trampled someone's garden. When he got back to the elevators, it was Reuben who found your pa. It shook him up pretty bad. Shook us all up."

The Cincinnati rain is still beating against my window, and the words Shim was speaking are still alive in my study, in my head. They were the first words in many that would follow, that would tell a story so much deeper, so much more horrible, that I find them still hard to comprehend. A teacher friend of mine, Henry Ottoman, came to my classroom one morning a few years ago with the alarming news that his wife of twenty-five years had left him. He was stunned into near stupidity. He grieved for a long time, telling me how it had come as a complete shock. Just days before they had appeared happy, and that he and his wife were making plans to take a trip to Quebec. And then, *my life was over*, he said. After that, he said, *nothing made sense anymore. Neither love nor hate.*

Such were the words that Shim spoke to me. I suddenly realized that some kind of thread had been unraveled, and the event of Norman

Witt's death had shaken this town to its core, and I, with my hatred, had stumbled into its midst. After a long year and a half, Henry Ottoman's wife came back, begging forgiveness. He said he forgave her, but that would be the best she got. My own story's ending would not be even that kind.

"I'd like to show you something, Sam," Shim said, pointing toward the door.

I followed him out, and together we walked back to where the award case was. He turned on a light switch beside the glass case and the interior was instantly lit up. Take a look at some of those photographs. The baseball ones."

Looking in, I saw a group of ragtag boys in uniform, some holding bats, the others just standing.

"State B champions. 1952, 1954 and 1957. Then a pause, until 1961 and 1963. That was just two years ago. That tall kid, number 11, in the fifty-two and fifty-five photos is Reuben Flett. Now, take a long look at the coach. He's standing at the far right."

I looked. There stood, in a baseball uniform, the mirror image of myself. Norman Witt.

"Now look at the 1963 championship team. Over here. There's your pop again, with Reuben as assistant coach."

It was like drinking poison. While I was playing ball in high school and college, trying to form a father-like relationship with my coaches, my own father was giving what I should have had to a whole team of somebody else's boys. My face turned white and Shim saw it.

"Don't take it too hard, son. I know something that I doubt even Reuben knows."

"I'm not sure I want to know, Mr. Harden."

"That's fine. It'll keep."

Staring at the photographs gave full evidence now as to why it was so easy to know who I was, even to the railroad clerk in Ritzville. From the eyebrows and eyes, to the nose and mouth, and even the angle of the chin, I was Norman Witt's son, and there was no mistaking it.

My appetite was gone, but I wanted to be shed of this place now too. I turned to Shim Harden and our eyes met.

"This town is no different than any other town, Sam. It has its secrets. Those who think they know, probably don't. If you care to find out what they are, you have to start by trusting no one."

I could only nod somberly.

Henry Ottoman was a good teacher. I felt rather privileged, in a backhanded sort of way, that he would trust me with his sad story, and at times, real tears. He adored his wife, and every day that their separation went on, he would continue to keep a prayerful vigil for the hope she would find a renewed affection for him. At times he passed through a wilderness of doubt, but steadfastly clung to a love he simply could not deny. He told me that he was working in the garden of the house he'd bought after the split, when he looked up one day and saw her standing by the gate. *I felt a stone fall out of my heart, Sam. In all those long months, I made a vow to always love her, no matter what. And that no matter her crimes against me, I would never do her harm.* Henry said when he saw her at the gate, he knew why she had come. *I took her in my arms, Sam, as if a broken child, and just held her. But in the end, it was all I could give her. Too much had passed.* It was clear that Henry had become a stronger man, to himself.

A saintly man, in spite of the outcome, Henry was a bigger man then me. Sure, he had chosen love over hate, he just knew love's limits.

Much to my relief, I found the cafe mostly empty. There were a couple of farmers in deep conversation about the price of wheat, and they hadn't even noticed my arrival. The pool room was silent. I sat on a stool at the counter and waited for a waitress. I could smell fried potatoes and the bitter smell of overcooked coffee. As I waited, another man entered and sat down at the far end of the counter. Turning, he looked across at me and stared, his expression growing into one of irritation, either at me, or at life in general.

"What'll you have?" came a friendly voice.

Looking up I saw it was the girl from yesterday afternoon, Oline on her name tag. Taking her in, I saw the same pretty face, though a bit serious.

"You need a menu?" But she didn't wait for an answer, instead she fetched one and passed it across. Glancing at it, I could feel her eyes on me. I looked up for a second and found her blue eyes penetrating me, so I looked away. There was no concentrating on the menu, so I just pointed to something and she asked if I wanted coffee.

"I just made a fresh pot," she said.

But she didn't move, so I looked up at her again. Her eyes are what spoke, their blueness as deep as river water, and they seemed to exude curiosity rather than the condemnation I was expecting.

"Are you here for long?"

I shook my head. "Not long. Just long enough to make enemies and then leave."

"Your father was well-liked here."

"So I've heard."

"I'll get your coffee." And she did. She was back with a filled cup and a spoon. She put cream and sugar in front of me, and turning, gave my order to the cook. But she wasn't done with me yet.

"You're sitting in the same place he sat every morning. And now it's you. Forgive me, but that's hard for me to connect with. All this. I hope you understand."

I was warming to her pretty face. There was no hostility in her words, only honesty. "Just me being here is hard to connect with," I said. "I'm finding out that the man I've hated my whole life was loved by everyone else."

"It's really none of my business. I just felt like saying something."

"Order up," the cook said.

Oline went to the window, picked up the plate and set it before me. It was two eggs, over medium, bacon and toast. I took a drink of coffee and she refilled it. Eventually she moved down the counter and took the order of the other man. I broke my eggs over my toast and forced myself to eat. Oline did not speak to me again, so I finished, left a tip and stepped down from the stool. At the other end of the counter the man looked at me again and sneered. The old fighter from the tenements put a hot current down my neck, but Shim Harden's words came back to me—*Those who think they know probably don't.* I forced myself to walk away.

Teaching history out of a textbook is like painting by numbers. The very thing most needed is interaction. If a teacher can get students to buy into discussion, then the whole business of history becomes a Lazarus moment, where conclusions find their own resurrections, and the danger of propaganda from remote historical scholars becomes less meddling. Too few of those scholars have walked the Great Plains, breathing in the air of Lewis and Clark, the mountain men, or even Laura Ingles Wilder. History requires experience.

All this I was to learn.

I decided I wasn't much interested in eating at the cafe anymore. Though Oline had shown no judgment, her words, nonetheless, were like bitter medicine. Leaving, I strode back up the hill to the cabin where I spent the better part of the day brooding. Nancy McGrath had still not returned from Ritzville, not that her presence would alter my mood. I was lonely, and even the storms of Mercedes would have been welcome. Better would have been the sweet face of Ashley.

Staring at the sea chest, I took the key from my pocket and fiddled with it. What could Norman Witt possibly have inside that box that would be of any interest to me? I tossed the key on top of the chest and laid back on the cot. Last night's attempt at sleep had been abysmal, and before I knew it, I was asleep.

In the warmth of that afternoon nap, dreams came to me, and as dreams go, they moved across a plain of nonsense, beginning with a vision of my classroom, empty of children, but with a naked Mercedes sitting in the back row. She was raising her hand, as if to answer a question, and her breasts jiggled like bowls of Jell-O. But instantly I was on the train again, sitting across from the old Montana woman, and she was shaming me for thinking of naked women. *If you're going to think about something, think about buffalo,* she said. But I didn't. Instead I saw the girl from the cafe. Oline. And her blue eyes seemed to be speaking directly to me—*I hope you understand.*

Muggy sweat covered my face and I blinked away my stupid fog of awakening. The pain of loneliness had not left me, and I felt surprisingly close to tears, even though my life in Cincinnati was no less lonely. In my life, outside of a handful of special moments with Ashley, I had never felt the full blossom of happiness.

Listening now to the rain on the window of my study, I no longer feel lonely, for my wife has been the wise and loyal person to fill my heart with joy. And I only hope that I have given her the same. She understands me, and understands the grief of what I learned in Eltopia, and she shows a gentleness that only God knows better. Hearing her in the other room, getting out of the tub, gives me a thrill of wellbeing, just knowing that once she is dressed she will ask me if I am ready for coffee. Routine is a life saver.

Shim Harden's circular saw was replaced now with a distant hammering, and I found myself envying his life. Next I heard the blue station wagon rumbling up the dirt road towards the post office. Sitting on the edge of my cot, I remembered the cookies she had given me. The breakfast I had eaten had settled like a lump in my stomach, so I took up the plate of cookies and slowly started eating.

As my mind replayed the night before, in Nancy McGrath's kitchen, with both our hands in the cookie dough, a small, overlooked image came back to me, something barely noticed at the time. It seemed odd that she would plunge her hands into a bowl of cookie dough, wearing a long sleeved blouse, but she did. And then, as we kneaded the dough, I remembered that the sleeve of her left arm hiked up just an inch or two, revealing what looked like the bottom of a scratch, still showing the signs of redness.

The image was soon gone when she began milking the dough from my fingers, one at a time, and laughing softly. It was the sensuousness of the moment that had erased it from my memory. But it was there now, and as I ate two more cookies, I felt the urge to know about it. If she invited me for supper again tonight, I would consider asking her. There was no mystery as to why I wanted to know. Nancy McGrath was a striking woman, and the more of her flesh she revealed, the less lonely I might feel. I had already glimpsed the smooth, white skin of her belly when she momentarily lifted her arms. But the scratch was something else.

There was a small bookshelf in the cabin, but no books, so I assumed they had been packed into the trunk. If I was to survive another night here, I might be forced to open the damn thing just to see if there was any kind of distracting literature in there. And yet, I was mildly curious about what kinds of books my father might have read. Was he a Mickey Spillane kind of guy? Travis McGee? Sherlock Holmes? I wouldn't know until I knew. So, I was just on the verge of giving in and opening the lock on the chest when there was a light knock on the door.

"It's me, Sam. Nancy. Can I come in?"

I nodded, knowing that wasn't an answer, so I said, "Yes. Come in." Secretly I was anxious for company. Any company.

When she opened the door, she was holding two bottles of Rainier, cold sweat formed on the amber necks.

"I hope you're thirsty. I don't drink much," she said, "but it's been one of those days, so I thought I might join you for a minute."

Taking one of the outstretched beers, I motioned to the chair by the little desk, and she sat. She had shed her postal uniform and was back in a pair of jeans and a print blouse. A long sleeved blouse. Her face seemed slightly flushed, perhaps from the warm day; perhaps from having just got done working; perhaps from being in the very room, where she may have visited often. For reasons unknown, only imagined.

"How was your day?" she asked.

I took a drink of beer and shrugged. "Nothing special."

"I see the lock is still on the trunk. You haven't opened it yet?"

I shook my head.

"Well, I guess there's time for that. Did you have lunch?"

Without a word, I motioned to the half-eaten cookies."

"Oh, Sam. Shame on you. You should have gone down to the cafe." Her voice had taken on a tone of familiarity, as if she was mothering me in an alluring kind of way.

"I had breakfast down there."

"Was it good?"

These were pointless questions, and I was now wondering what the whole point of her being here was. I didn't have long to wait.

"Actually, I put a stew on this morning and let it heat in the crockpot while I was gone. I hope you like roast beef."

"Is this an invitation?"

Nancy McGrath laughed, and her face became almost beautiful. "It could be. But I'd rather call it a direct order."

We both drank from our bottles of beer. There was something about the heat coming in from the open door, the time of the day, and the faint smell of lavender that was coming from some unknown place that came close to dizzying me. I recognized it to be intimacy. As much as I hated the thought of it, I could not blame my father for whatever liberties he may have had with this woman. Nancy McGrath was in full command.

Eventually I remembered the scratch on her arm, but by that time I could have cared less. I felt I was being saved from utter boredom by this woman, and I would take what I could get of it until Friday when the train stopped in Eltopia again. But who was she? I remembered someone saying she had taken over the postal duties that her father had kept for thirty years. So, was she a local girl, following her father around until the day she picked up the gauntlet? She seemed, in a peculiar way, to own this little town. And why not? She had access to everyone's mail, which amounted to knowing about weddings, childbirths, bankruptcies, foreclosures, all based on the letters delivered and the reaction by the people receiving them.

We sat in something close to embarrassment, considering we were total strangers creeping around the edges of flirtation. A blade of grass had stuck to the top of her shoe, and as she bent forward to pluck it off, I could see past her buttoned blouse to her tan neck and beyond, to where a view of her cleavage was on display. She glanced up as she bent and saw me looking, but she made no effort to straighten up. My vast experience with Mercedes told me what the intent of this was. She was a woman, after all, and she still had her weapons.

Almost as quickly as she came, she stood and left. "Supper is at six, Sam. Just knock on the door, and then come in. That way I know it's you."

I watched her walk across the lawn.

My second supper with Nancy McGrath was a replay of the night before, with her playing the perfect, if not somewhat nervous hostess. We sat across from each other and I watched her carefully, looking for signs of unease, like the mild shaking of her hands that I'd seen before. I tried to engage her in personal conversation, asking her once about her childhood, to which I received a shake of her head and a mere, *oh, just a small town girl*.

The stew was tasty and I found that I had an appetite for the first time since arriving in Eltopia. In truth, I was finding her company refreshing, and I became relaxed, as she talked about the approaching summer and the hopes of finally having a garden. Nancy McGrath did not strike me as being a gardener, nor of someone who even concerned herself with the changing seasons. She was too intent on being the postmistress. So I counted this as a means of keeping the conversation simple, and away from questions about herself.

As we cleared the table of our dirty dishes, we stood side by side at the sink, and there again, like before, the long sleeve of her blouse rode up, revealing the bottom of that red scratch. On an impulse, I reached out and circled her wrist with my hand, not hard, but somewhat firmly.

"What's this?" I said.

She started to pull away, but then stopped, and we looked at her arm together. Taking a further risk, I reached out with my other hand

and pushed the sleeve up higher, exposing the long, red abrasion. There it was, but alongside the main cut were two other, shorter ones.

"You've been hurt," I said, sympathetically.

"Oh. That. Just...Bob Granger's rooster. It's a vicious beast."

Our eyes met, but I still held her wrist, more gently now. And then, without invitation, I stroked the length of her injured arm with my hand in an effort to show comfort. Something in my touch made her quiver and I saw her eyes close for just a moment, as if getting a kind of unexpected pleasure from my soothing affection. We stood like that, unmoving for a long moment, until she took a breath and said, "Oh, Sam."

Finally she moved my hand away and pulled her sleeve back down, but I saw in her face a blush of both surprise and desire. She breathed deeply and even I could feel the very real threshold that was opening between us. One word, I feared, and we would be in each other's arms, with only our natural needs to take us deeper. Was I ready for this? I turned away, taking a step towards the table. There sat our empty drinking glasses, and grabbing them both I stood, facing her now at a safer distance. But Nancy McGrath was slow to recover, and I knew that one or the other of us was the spider. Still, looking at her face, and her lips, which now did show a bit of a quiver, I wanted her. But it was she, finally, who turned away, plunging her hands into the soapy water of the sink. When she reached up to swipe at a lock of her blonde hair, I saw the return of that mild shaking of her hand.

Men can be easily manipulated sometimes. It's usually later that the shame of it perches on our better judgment, and we feel the part of a fool. Our needs are like clay in the hands of the wrong women, and the price we pay, in the end, can be devastating. What was the price Norman Witt had paid? I did not even consider this until after our second supper together in Nancy McGrath's kitchen was over, where I managed to escape unscathed. But later, in seeking some fresh air, I let the night replay itself as I chose to walk down towards the railway yard, and an empty train car parked like a lonesome talisman in the night.

It wasn't completely dark; a beautiful scarlet gloaming had stretched across the horizon above the surrounding buttes. It was only in hindsight that I was able to see this as a preordained appointment with destiny. Had I not done that uncharacteristic venture of wandering down the hill for a breath of evening air, my whole time in Eltopia, and assuredly my entire life afterwards, would have been impossibly different. As I was to learn, God's gentle hand of teaching isn't always gentle.

From the darkening corner of the rail car, a shadow appeared, followed by a voice.

"You," the voice said.

Had I been in the tenements again, I would have shown no fear, but here I was in hostile territory, and so I stiffened from genuine fright.

"Who's there?" It was a weak reply.

"You know who I am."

I swallowed. "Reuben Flett?"

The shadow approached and I could see a braided Indian before me, his long arms at ease at his sides, his jeans and boots alone exuding confidence. "Why have you come? So late? Norman waited for you. And now you come when he is dead."

I felt I was talking to a voice and not a person, as his deeper features remained shaded by the twilight.

"I never came because Norman Witt is a son of a bitch."

The blow came so fast I didn't even feel it until I was on my back in the dust and weeds. I shook my head, then quickly, already filling with that old fatherless rage, I sprang to my feet. But Reuben Flett, in a jumble of moves, put a knuckled fist against my eye and I could feel the blood instantly. I swung and missed, and with open hands Reuben Flett pushed me onto the ground again. This was something different altogether than the many fights I had been in. I debated whether to get up again, but I did, and this time it was a solid punch to my chest that felt like my heart had suddenly stopped. I sat on the ground, gasping.

"You are the son of a bitch, Sam Witt."

"Whadda you know?" I choked out.

"I know what you don't know. Tomorrow I will twist your lies into truths. Be at this very place at first light. Class will be in session."

And just like that, Reuben Flett was a shadow again, having disappeared.

For a long time I sat there on the ground, my chest aching. I had just had my ass kicked, and I could barely remember any of it. I put my hand to my eye and felt the blood. For a minute I fought back against nausea, but eventually I got to my feet. I had lost all sense of direction, and so I staggered blindly up the hill, my head down, the blood dripping into my eye. At some point, coming out of the tall grass and onto the main road, I saw a series of concrete blocks for the foundation of an old, long gone building had set, and I sat down again.

I was looking down at my shoes when I heard a door open and then close. Glancing up I saw that I was close to the cafe, the lights out. From the closed door a shadow came down the steps, the second shadow I had seen that night, and I stiffened. It came in my direction but not at me. But suddenly I heard a gasp, and in a moment of abandoned clarity, I found myself staring into the astonished face of Oline, the waitress.

"What happened to you?" she said.

Taking a breath, I mumbled something.

"Good grief, Sam. You're bleeding. Get up. Come on. Let's get back inside. I'll try and fix you up."

She took my hand and I followed her, without argument, back into the cafe.

"Sit down," she commanded.

Oline was gone for a minute and when she returned she placed a wet cloth against my eye. "Hold that while I get some bandages."

Beyond shame, I sat there. A narrow thread of light knifed through the room, enough to see her coming back. The light gave her the look of an angel, and I remembered Henry Ottoman's words, about how his wife looked the day she entered his garden gate.

Oline went to work, tearing tape and laying out a piece of gauze. "Who did this to you?"

"I fell."

"I'm sure you did. After being knocked down."

"It doesn't matter. It was a difference of opinion."

"Who started it?"

"I...I guess I might have."

"It was Reuben, wasn't it? Nobody else in this stinking town would have the guts to do it."

"Dead men tell not tales."

"But you're not dead." Oline's voice was growing testy.

"My father is though."

She didn't say another word until she had stopped the bleeding and taped a piece of gauze above my eye. When she was done she sat on the floor in front of me, and her blue eyes managed to penetrate the dim light of the cafe. "If you came to Eltopia looking for trouble, Sam Witt, you certainly found it."

"I'm not sure anymore why I came here."

"Why did Reuben hit you?"

I tried to meet her stare but I lost my courage. "I called my father a son of a bitch."

"Oh. Well, I might have hit you too."

"There's two sides to every story."

"And which side have you forgotten. The side you don't want to hear."

Putting my hands on my knees, I started to stand up, but Oline pushed me back into the chair. "Not so fast, mister. By the looks of it, I might be the only friend you have."

Looking at her now, I said, "Could I touch your hand?"

"Why?"

I shrugged. "I don't know. I just want to touch your hand."

She put her hand out and I took it and gently held it, as if it were an offering of rose pedals. It felt warm to the touch and inside of it I felt a current of amity, just as she had said. "I need a friend."

"Well, you can start by not thinking your side of the story is the only side."

Oline did not remove her hand and so I said, "I'll try."

"If you let me go, I'll make a pot of coffee. And if you're a gentleman, you can tell me your side of the story."

I let her hand go, and I watched her move through the dimness to the coffee maker.

Is it ironic that at this very moment, in my study, I can hear my wife asking from the kitchen if I want coffee? Of course I do, and of course I tell her. By now though, it is her company I want more. She is the one person that I have always been able to count on. She reads my moods, which, by the way, are not always gloomy as now, but the death of friends brings sadness to the surface.

After we were married for a year, and we had saved a little bit of money, we went on a belated honeymoon to Boston. For me it was an extension of this new method of teaching I had adopted, so walking through old Boston was like walking back into the ages of time. I felt every bit the tourist, while my wife seemed more at home, more relaxed, having gotten both the history connection, but also the literary fulfilment of touring the homes of Louisa May Alcott, Edith Wharton, and Herman Melville's Arrowhead, where he wrote *Moby Dick*. On the way back we drove through Virginia, where we stopped at Thomas Jefferson's Monticello, and it was here that she fell in love with gardening. Jefferson's perfectly plotted beds of living vegetables, herbs and flowers, were a delight to her inner senses, for which has remained in her attempts to duplicate Jefferson's work in our backyard.

We moved to a booth in the cafe and Oline sat across from me, our coffee like a peace treaty between us. In the quiet and the warmth of the night, I pieced together the story of my life as a fatherless child in post war Cincinnati. Of course, I left out some of my dumber escapades, sticking as close as possible to the feelings of worthlessness that I often felt, even more worthless then those boys whose fathers were actually killed in the war. At least they had an honorable excuse.

Oline listened, as true as she had promised, saying little, but with an occasional sigh of empathy, which came out in a soft breath, of which I found myself trying to inhale for the medicine it felt like. We finished the entire pot of coffee before she asked me again about Reuben Flett.

"What did he say to you?"

I tried to remember his words. "He...he wants me to meet him in the morning. He said he wanted to untwist my lies." I watched Oline's eyes as she took this in, their blueness like a drug, and I saw a sadness for the first time.

"He probably wants to kick my butt again."

"I don't think so," she said, her voice gentle. "Reuben may be the one person in this hick town that misses your father more than all the others put together. I know Reuben better than most around here, and I'd wager you've seen the worst of him. From here on you might be surprised."

My head was hurting now, but I kept my eyes on her. "Are you saying I should meet him?"

"What else did he say?"

"Something about class being in session."

"Then yes. I think you should go."

It was nearing midnight already, and I had learned, in just one day, that first light could happen any minute now. "I've kept you up late, listening to my sad tale."

"It was my idea. Remember. Besides, tomorrow is my day off, so I can sleep in."

"Where do you live, if you don't mind me asking?"

"I might mind," she said, smiling. "But I'll tell you anyway. I live on my aunt and uncle's farm, about a mile up the canyon. I'm a big girl now, so I won't get a lecture for being home late. Besides, they're heavy sleepers."

We stood at the same time and she walked me to the door, where I turned to face her. "You saved me tonight, Oline. I'm indebted to you, and I don't even have the means to repay you."

"Just stay out of trouble. That'll be repayment enough."

I hesitated, not wanting to go, but she'd asked me beforehand to be a gentleman, and so I left, dragging myself up the hill and into the cabin, where I managed to fall asleep fully clothed.

———————

My wife is doing her hair and I am drinking my coffee in my study, still in my pajamas and robe, putting off what is to be a long plane ride from Cincinnati to Spokane, followed by a rental car that I will drive back to the town where ghosts live, even a partial ghost of myself. It feels like I am John Donner in Conrad Richter's classic, *The Waters of Kronos*, where he finds himself returning to Unionville, a town that is no more, having been swallowed up by a newly formed lake. But Donner finds himself taken back in time, on the day of his grandfather's funeral, to be reunited with a long lost time. And here I am, Sam Witt, going back to a town filled with a mountain of memories, to bury my friend Reuben Flett. It weighs so heavy on my heart that I fear I may break down.

It was the rooster, Bob Granger's rooster, roaming the field where a handful of chickens strutted among the sheep pasture that woke me up with its crowing, my head splitting as by a Viking axe. Still dressed, I cursed the day and my life, and the lapse of good sense that brought me here. I skipped a shower, simply splashing water on my face. My hair was a mess, so I put my head under the spigot and then ran my fingers through its thick mop, the bandage over my eye remaining affixed. I decided I was doing this only because Oline said I should, otherwise I would be sleeping off my battered brain.

I made the railway car just as the first blade of dawn broke over the mesa. And there he was, Reuben Flett, the Indian, standing straight as a ramrod, and holding the reins of two horses. He said nothing as I approached, only handed me the reins of one of the horses, a shiny brown animal, as he quietly mounted his own.

"I've never ridden a horse before."

"Well, it does not take a genius. Put your foot in the stirrup and swing your leg over. Surely you've seen John Wayne movies, he the killer of many Hollywood Indians." Reuben's voice was level, free of humor, but not hostile, which surprised me. He made no mention of the bandage over my eye. That would come later.

"We'll go slowly so you don't fall off. By the time we get back your legs and ass are going to hurt like hell. That's the price of being a tinhorn."

Reuben Flett led the way out of town at a canter, crossing the main road and up again on a worn dirt path that took us to the top of a ridge. The inside of my legs already felt chaffed and it had only been ten minutes. Up and over we went, and looking back I could see the smudge of a town, and in a peculiar way I was glad I was leaving it, even for this bizarre expedition with an angry native Indian. It seemed a long ride with no words spoken between us, just Reuben leading the way ten yards ahead, over a broad landscape of wild grass and sagebrush and rim rock. Indeed it did resemble a John Wayne movie, one or more, filmed on location in a place much like this. We eventually passed down through a rocky ravine and I drew my horse up next to his.

"Where are we going?" I asked.

"Badger Lake."

"What's at Badger Lake?"

"You ask too many questions."

We rode wordlessly for another half an hour, until finally, just visible through the basalt arroyos, the shimmer of a blue lake came into view. Our horses seemed to know the way as much as Reuben Flett did, and the smell of water reached us, something like a mirage in the desert. As we rode, single file again, I noticed a grassy flat to the right of the narrow trail, and it seemed we were headed towards that. My backside ached.

Reuben motioned to stop, and taking a long look around, he finally dismounted, so I did the same.

"Keep your ears and eyes open for rattlesnakes," he said.

My senses immediately went on high alert, my eyes suddenly taking in every inch around me. There was a post in the ground with a big ring on it and Reuben tied the reins to the ring, and with a nod of his head indicated that I do the same. From there he led me to the edge of the grassy area where several boulders were strewn, and he sat on one, motioning for me to sit on the other one.

Reuben didn't speak for a long time, but finally he said, "You and me. We share two different kinds of pain."

"What do you know about my pain?"

"I know it, because it was the same pain your father had."

"You brought me all the way out here to insult me?"

Reuben Flett turned to me and for the first time, in the sunlight, I was able to study his features, his noble nose, his long Indian braids, his tan skin, the denim jeans and the long-sleeved olive green shirt. He wore no hat and he wore no feathers as I stupidly imagined he might. But there was a chain around his neck with a carved wooden cross at the end.

"It is a shame that your mind is closed to the truth."

"My truth is my truth," I said, angrily.

Reuben gave a light laugh, shaking his head. "In many ways you are just like him."

"I doubt that."

He laughed again. "And still you talk like a fool."

"Fine," I said. "Then let's get to the point of this whole venture."

Nodding, Reuben went on. "Norman Witt saved me from myself. When I was just a boy."

"So I heard."

"Be quiet and listen."

Below us, on the lake, a group of ducks were swimming contentedly among the reeds. And small birds would light on the heads of cattails, bending the shafts sideways, until they flew away.

"It wasn't really me he wanted to save. Not in the beginning. It was you. You were all he talked about. His little Sammy. Whom he had never gotten to know while he was in the war. But wanted desperately to know you now."

It was easy to see the pain this Indian was feeling as he spoke. He would take long pauses, sometimes so long I thought he had said all he was going to say, but eventually he'd pick up the narrative again.

"Norman came out to work on the dam. The Grand Coulee Dam, which was the big employer of workers, even after it was finished. People, like your father, who were hard workers, never lacked for work. And it was his dream to send for your mother, sister and you, so that you could live a better life out here."

"He told you all this?"

"Norman got hurt on the job, in nineteen forty-eight. So he used his GI bill to go to school in Pullman. It was Washington State College back then. He earned his engineering degree and started working in the towns to the south of here. Pasco and Kennewick. But the pain from his injury made it hard to do some of the long hours of work. When the shop teacher here took a job in Walla Walla, Norman was asked to replace him. And so he did."

"My father was a teacher?"

"And then he took a bunch of scrap dog kids, like me, and started coaching the baseball team. I was too young at first, so he made me a bat boy. But it was his dream to bring you out and have you on the team."

"Then why didn't he?"

"He tried. Three times Norman left here and went back to Cincinnati. To get you."

"That's not true. I never saw him once."

"You are showing your ignorance again, Sam Witt."

I stood. "I don't believe any of this. You're just full of stories."

Reuben sat calmly, watching me stomp around. Finally he said, "Each time he came back he was in a bad way. Depressed for weeks. We lost three straight games, which cost us the championship that year. All because he came back empty handed."

Turning, I faced him. "If he came back to get me, why didn't he?"

"The letters would have explained that."

"What letters?"

"The letters he wrote you." Reuben had finally begun to show some emotion. He stood and circled the boulder he'd been sitting on. "Hundreds of them, Sam. Hundreds. I saw him writing them myself. As much as I loved him, I knew that I was not his son. You were."

I stood, stunned. "No letters ever came for me." Our eyes met, and there was questioning in both our faces. The sun was making a rising arc in the sky now, and it was throwing a shadow over our shoulders. And then the face of my mother appeared in my mind and I wondered, *Could her hatred have run that deep?*

"There's more," Reuben said, his voice almost too quiet to hear.

I was in mourning for myself again, trying hard to make sense of the insensible, but none of this added up and I feared my head might explode from the effort.

Thinking back on this moment from my study, I remembered Henry Ottoman's words, when his wife first left him. *It was like looking at a mannequin, Sam. I just didn't know her.* Here now, if Reuben Flett's words were true, then who really was Norman Witt?

"What else?" I said.

He put a stare on me that nearly froze me. "This can never be spoken of. It is *really* a criminal offense."

"Making me an accessory?"

"Not in the act. Only in the truth."

Reuben pointed towards a gap in the basalt ridge where we sat, and looking, I saw a small pile of stones I hadn't noticed before. "Your father's ashes, in a boxed urn."

"What?"

"I think you should sit back down for this. I don't want to have to answer any of your questions until I get it all out."

I could not take my eyes off the little pile of stones, seeing now that they were stacked neatly. He motioned again for me to sit, and so I finally did.

Reuben looked up at the sky, as if trying to gain strength from some old Indian god, but then I remembered the cross around his neck, and it added all the more to the confusion.

"I am not a suspicious man by nature. My beliefs tell me that there is a design to everything. But your father's death left too many questions. Questions, that at the time, no one seemed interested in answering. Your father was helping out at the grain warehouse that day. A kid had come down and told me that my horses had broken out of their corral and so I left to catch them. Your father was working on the highest floor, bagging some oats that the mice had chewed into. It's a long way up there. Forty feet or more. We used an old rope elevator to pull ourselves up and down."

At this point Reuben had to stop, and he turned away from me, and it was at this point that he was suffering from Norman Witt's death, more than I was. There would come a time, soon enough, for my own grief. While Reuben's sadness was passing, I stared down at the rock grave and an odd sensation crossed over me, as if his ashes somehow had my name on them. If they could speak to me, I wondered what they might say.

Reuben picked up a small rock and threw it far into the lake, where it left a silent splash and a circle of ripples. "They buried Norman in the little cemetery on the hill. The one with an old wire fence around it, and a mess of overgrown weeds."

"What? But...you just said those were his ashes."

"They are." He was facing me again. "They buried a coffin holding two gunny sacks of prime red wheat."

I put my hands to my head. "What are you talking about? This isn't making any sense."

"It will. Just listen." He held up his hand to quiet me. "I stole Norman's body. That's my crime. Body snatching is a criminal offence."

"One of us is hallucinating." I shook my head.

"Almost from the moment your father was dead, Nancy McGrath had two farm boys out in the cemetery digging a grave. They worked till dark, making that hole. So she had your father's coffin put in that cabin. The one you're sleeping in."

My head fell in disbelief.

"Things were going too fast. Way too fast. I didn't like it. There was no mention of a funeral. No anything."

"So you stole my father's body? You're not serious."

"He was wrapped in a blanket already, so I jimmied the door to the cabin after midnight. I'm an Indian, so I know how to be quiet. My people were famous horse stealers."

"Reuben. I think you are a crazy Indian. I mean, legitimately crazy. Like lunatic crazy."

Reuben ignored this. "I have friends up at the Colville reservation. They work in a lab up there. Once in a while they'll do an autopsy on a body. Or they'll call somebody in to do it. One that didn't just die from drunk driving. If it was a gunshot wound, or a disease, or something serious like that, they'll take a look. But there was something fishy about this whole thing. And why the big hurry to put your father in the ground? It just didn't make any sense. Something was being covered up."

It was my turn to pick up a rock and toss it far out into the water. "You drove my dead father from Eltopia to that place, up there, wherever you said. Because you wanted them to do an autopsy?"

Reuben nodded.

"And now you're going to tell me what they found, right?"

"Of course, the cause of death was obvious. He died from the fall. Head and body trauma. It was instant."

"And, what else?"

"They didn't catch it at first, but after they looked at everything more closely, they found something very strange."

I waited.

"Human skin under his fingernails."

In my study, the rain is coming down harder, in sheets, and I can hear it, filling my ears with a sound like machine gun fire, the sounds my father heard from the time he went off to help save the world, until the victory. But even over the drumming of the rain, I continue to hear Reuben's words, and they carried a devastating punch, worse than any fight I was ever in. *Human flesh under his fingernails.* I tried to back away from the words, but I could not do it. Their impact was immediate.

One of the horses nickered impatiently and we both looked. A long, soundless moment passed between Reuben and me, as if an unknown truth had suddenly been made known. When our eyes finally met, I saw the honor of this man, and the loyalty he showed a man I had hated my entire life. Reuben Flett was proving himself a much better man than me.

"Nancy McGrath has scratches on her arm," I said, my words flying out like bats from a cave.

Reuben's dark eyes leveled at me. "Have you seen this?"

"Yes. I told you. I saw them. One long one and two shorter ones. As if..." There was no need to finish.

"How did she get them? Did she say?"

I nodded. "Bob Granger's rooster."

He shook his head. "I...I had the doctor record his findings. That there was flesh under Norman's nails. Of course, there's no way of proving it was Nancy McGrath's flesh, but..." Reuben looked out at the lake and a soft wave of ripples was running its length like the melody of a song. "They kept a copy of the report, and they gave me one too. So I had...I had Norman cremated. I wanted him to come to rest."

We both looked down at the pile of stones.

"That explains the rush to have him buried," he said.

"So you think it might be a match? His fingernails and her scratches?"

"It has to be."

I was beginning to feel the same. "Tell me, Reuben. Were they lovers? Nancy McGrath and my father?"

Reuben sat down on his boulder again and motioned for me to do the same. "We need to talk about all this. There are a lot of pieces and now I think some of them are starting to fit together."

I sat, but asked again, "We they lovers?"

"Well, he lived there. In her cabin. At least the last several years. But Norman belonged to the town, Sam. Not just to her. He belonged to the school. To the baseball team. If anyone needed a hand, he was there. He was even there for me the day he died. Helping out while I went chasing after my damn horses. Who really knows? There wasn't any public display of it, if that's what you're asking. Nancy McGrath is brutally private. She is a woman of secrets."

And wiles, I thought.

"Your father wasn't even fifty years old. He had a lot of life left in him. He worked around the pain in his back from when he fell at the dam. What put him in her cabin, once he moved in, is anybody's guess. And if there were incentives—like sex—well, who could blame him."

No words came to me, so I just nodded, remembering how easy it might have been just the night before, to grab Nancy McGrath and have my way with her. Or would it have been *her* way?

"I want to find out, Sam. I don't think he fell. I believe he was pushed."

Nancy McGrath's words came back to me. *Reuben Flett is someone to stay away from. He's trouble.*

But how could someone, so adored by my father, be trouble. My father, according to everything I had heard so far, was the very person who saved young Reuben *from* trouble. He turned him into a baseball player of superior high school quality. He taught Reuben how to box, and box with skill, as the scar above my eye testifies to this day.

Between the pages of one of my favorite books—Remarque's *A Night in Lisbon*—is a photograph of Reuben and I together. It was taken by the waitress Oline the day before I was set to leave back to Cincinnati. He and I were sitting on the bench outside of the cafe, and Oline, with a borrowed camera, caught an image of the two of us in calculated conversation. Much of what we'd set out to do remained unfinished, and it showed in the photo as heartache.

Even now, in my study, so many years later, it is still heartache, some of what has been partially winnowed away by time and by justice, but the reality of that truth my father wrote of, remains. *Memory is not always the same as truth.* It took Eltopia to make me understand that.

It was time to look inside Norman Witt's sea chest.

A small chink in my armor of hatred for my father had taken place, inflicted by the decency and trustworthiness of the Indian, Reuben Flett. My pain of abandonment remained piercing, but I was beginning to see a new, albeit, confusing new side to this stranger-father. There were pieces missing in this story and at least now, I was interested in finding out what they were.

We stayed at Badger Lake into late afternoon, Reuben relaying stories of who Norman Witt was, and at the heart of it, according to him, was myself, the boy he loved. Even though he didn't know me, he apparently wanted to. I likewise gave Reuben a glimpse into my oftentimes wayward life in the wild streets of post war Cincinnati. Some of the things Reuben told me were hard pills to swallow, of the so-called three times Norman returned from Ohio, supposedly to fetch me, only to be brokenhearted. How could this have happened? That he would come to see me and leave empty handed? Was it even true?

The only person who could confirm it was my mother, and at this place in my life, and hers, I wondered if she'd even care to remember. Or, if she did remember, to tell the truth.

Reuben had left me off at the same place he had picked me up, leading the horses back to his place. Nancy McGrath was in the post office when I returned, so I hoped to arrive unnoticed, only because I was not in the mood for explanations about where I'd been, and with who. If she was as knowing as folks in Eltopia said of her, then she likely had figured it out already.

I sat on my bunk, staring at the trunk for a long time, fidgeting with the key. What would I find in there? I feared it might be letters unsent. Letters he had written in front of people just for show, to make him look like something he wasn't, someone who missed his son. The answers were behind that lock and under that lid and so I was steadying myself for that discovery. But before I could make a move, I saw a shadow pass along a side window, and there was the unmistakable blonde head of Nancy McGrath, moving across the backyard. I stood, and going to the window I watched as she crossed the grass and moved toward the little shed that was the pump house. Leaning against the wall of the cabin, I could still see her at an angle through the window. She was carrying something, and then I saw her take a key from the back pocket of her jeans, insert it into a lock on the door. It swung part way, revealing a dark interior, and she disappeared inside, but in half a minute she was out again, locking the door and moving back across the lawn. She was no longer carrying anything.

Fearing detection, my only hope was to feign a nap, so I stretched out on the cot with my back to the window, in case she peered in, and lay still, breathing the steady cadence of sleep. I waited long enough, to be sure she was gone, and then went back to the window. There was no sign of her. Angling my view through the window again, I stared at the shed. Even in the daylight, it possessed an ominous aura and I felt a shiver along my arms and neck, in spite of the warm afternoon.

It was back to the business of the trunk now, and so I opened it quickly. It was easy to see that Norman Witt had not filled this space with unsent letters, though what it did contain was mostly a legitimacy of the stories I had heard about him—two baseballs, a worn, leather glove and an equally well-used catcher's mitt, a ball cap with an embroidered E on the front, a dozen books, some mysteries, some westerns, among others, and clothes, well folded, either by Norman himself, or Nancy McGrath, before or after his death. There was a tablet too, with two ink pens, bound together by a rubber band, and a single framed photograph, black and white, of Staff Sergeant Norman Witt, standing in front of a bomb-blasted building, an M-1 rifle slung over his shoulder, with part of a Pershing tank taking up space on the side of the frame. He looked cold and his gloved hand was holding a cigarette.

Here was all that remained for me to understand the man who'd left me.

I thumbed through the book titles, wondering if anything he might have read would resonate with me and my own reading tastes. Only one, a hardback copy of *A Moveable Feast*, a book barely six months old. Of course, Hemingway himself was already dead these four years, but the memoir itself contained some of the writer's most tender offerings.

It was, once again, Mercedes who gave me the book, as a late Christmas present. In her circle, in Chicago, Hemingway was something of a hero to the yachting set, and since Chicago was the writer's birthplace, it seemed a fitting gift. I read it immediately, partly because Mercedes was hovering over me in expectance, but mostly because it was a fascinating read, as every lit class I had in college required reading at least one of Hemingway's books. I had managed *To Have and Have Not* one year, and the gloomy and angry *Across the River and Into the Trees* in my senior year.

But to discover that my father had read *A Moveable Feast* seemed somehow strange. I thumbed the pages, expecting to find dirty fingerprints, but each page was clean and neat. But on the last page, a small note fell out and landed in my lap. Picking it up I stared at what he had written—*I need to send this to Sam. Wonder what he thought of the others.*

I felt another chill creep up my back to my neck, colder even than the first. Was I the Sam he was talking about? And what others? I never got a single letter from him in my entire life, much less a book. What was he talking about? Was this just more of his blusters? Did he know he was going to die, and he just wrote this note to save face?

I started to put the book back in the trunk, but then changed my mind and put it under the pillow on my cot. I would show it to Reuben. Maybe he would know who this Sam was. We had agreed to meet later that night anyway, down by the railcar again. He wanted to take me up to the top of the grain elevator. We were still looking for answers.

But as I was rearranging the items back in the trunk, I found something that had gotten shoved under a pair of shirts. It was a grocery sack, partially full of something, but folded over and taped down. I picked it up, testing its weight. The tape was yellowed and tore away easily. I moved to the cot and dumped the contents out on the blanket. Letters. Easily two dozen or more. The envelopes were thin, single sheets at best. I picked one up and nearly staggered on my feet. My head instantly went light, as if short of oxygen. It was addressed to our tenement house, number 7, in Cincinnati. And it was sealed. It had never been opened.

I checked another, and another. They were all the same, all the familiar V-Mail envelopes furnished by the military, written by the GI's, then reproduced onto microfilm and then recopied and printed and sent to the states. I had seen a few, ones my friends showed me that their fathers had sent. Strange that I had never seen any from my father. I looked at the pile of letters, at the twisted art of them lying there, some envelopes showing the dullness of age. I picked each one up, turning them over, but not a single one had been opened. Why? If they were sent to us, from say North Africa, or Italy or Germany, why had they not been opened and read? Read to me and Shirley.

A picture of my mother started filling the cabin, like a panorama of bitterness, and I could only guess at the cause—she had been so filled with hatred that she despised even the words written in his hand. The hatred that filled her veins had poisoned her heart. There could be no other explanation. I held one to my nose, but it had no smell, only age. Could I bear to open one, considering all I had learned today? Was I strong enough for this now too? I tore the seal on one and removed the V-Letter—

...we are holding up in a barn, I can't tell you where exactly, only that we are in France. This village has been torn apart for the second time in twenty years.

We had it bad yesterday. We lost two good men, one killed, the other wounded and sent back to a medical station. There's no safe place though. There was a dead horse in the barn when we got here so I ordered it removed. The platoon is mine for now, our lieutenant getting killed two days ago...

It was my father talking. I could hear his voice, coming back through the years.

Hemingway's *A Moveable Feast* is one of a half dozen books I've read more than once. In fact, after reading it twice over a twenty year span, my wife and I listened to the audio version again just last summer on a road trip to the east coast. I found myself listening wordlessly for many hours, driving, imagining it was my father's story, even his voice, part criticism but mostly the tender remembrances of a youthful age when almost every American man was doing the same thing—fighting in a war that was so big that the rest of human existence seemed to vanish in comparison. Like Hemingway's, the memories of our youth—even my own—are rarely ones we could take an oath on. They are our tainted perspective of days long past.

The book I found in my father's trunk in Eltopia sits on my shelf before me now and I am tempted, with this memory, to pull it down, but there is no time. My wife is in the shower and I can smell the coffee all the way from the kitchen. Still, it is my own moveable feast that draws me back again to this time, when Reuben Flett was still young and very much alive, and meeting him at the empty train car after dark, it is like a crack in time, one to creep back into for one last time.

Reuben was not waiting for me this time, so leaning in the shadows, my mind returned to Nancy McGrath, and her unusual trip to the so-called pump house. Had seeing my father's urn out in the middle of the prairie rocks, and listening to Reuben's story, about human skin under Norman's fingernails, sparked in me the beginning of a suspicious mind? Was I now starting to question every movement that the postmistress made? I wasn't sure I wanted to believe her guilty of anything.

My thoughts were interrupted by Reuben's shadow, walking along the tracks, his head down as if in a well of thought. I had absolutely no understanding of such things as wheat warehouses and elevators, outside of the fact that they stood like miniature skyscrapers in this barren country and that even in the darkness there was something foreboding about them. At least about this one, considering it was the place of my father's death.

Without a word, we moved silently towards it. Reuben put a key in a lock that held a chain across the huge, aluminum sliding door and opened it just wide enough to squeeze inside. It was dark and the air was still settling with the day's frequent stirring of dust and wheat chaff.

"If you work here, why are we coming back like this?" I said this in a hushed voice. "You've had over two weeks to look this thing over."

"Two reasons," he said. "First, I want you to see it. I want you to get a feeling for what happened. And you have to go up to the top to understand."

Okay. I could accept that. "What's the second reason?"

"I didn't know about Nancy McGrath's scratches on her arm until you told me this morning. I need to take in that information from up there, not down here." He flipped a switch on the wall and a bare bulb blinked on, casting a further image of settling dust in the air. "The lift is over here. It's just a wooden platform with a rope. It's prehistoric.

You pull the rope and the weight on the other end lifts you and the platform up. I'll go first. I'll send it back down for you."

He stepped on the platform, pulled on the rope, and I watched him disappear into the darkness above. I waited, and after a minute the platform returned, so I stepped aboard and the process was repeated. It was a surreal ascent through a narrow darkness. Once I felt a cobweb brush my face, and I swiped at it, fearing spiders. When the platform had reached the top, Reuben grabbed my arm and helped me step into another dim room, lit only by another bare bulb. Inside and to the left were rows of gunny sacks, filled with grain and tied-off on top with twine. A stuffiness filled my nostrils and I sneezed.

"I'm leaving the lift up. Because I believe it was up when Norman fell. But look here. You see, if someone came up here to talk to him, the lift would have been up. And yet...there is still plenty of room to the side of the platform to fall down the shaft. So if someone, like Nancy McGrath, was up here. And let's say she did push Norman, there is space enough for him to fall without landing on the lift's platform. He would have fallen all the way down with the lift still up. Is any of this making sense to you?"

There was passion rising in Reuben's voice, so I peered over the edge of the room's opening and saw that he was correct. A body could easily have fallen without the lift being in the way. I nodded.

"So, what would have brought her, or anybody up here?" Reuben looked at me for a hypothetical.

Here was a puzzle. A dangerous puzzle, one based purely on speculation. "Okay," I said, considering. "Let's say, for the sake of simplicity, that it was Nancy McGrath. I would have to know more about their relationship. Can you answer that, Reuben? Was she and my father lovers?"

Reuben's eyes fell on me, and even in the dim light, they shown like diamonds. "After Norman's last accident. He fell coming out of a boxcar. He was sweeping it out, and he stepped backwards out the open door. It wrenched his back, which was already an issue. That was over two years ago. Nancy McGrath stepped in and made up that cabin for him. It was her chance. Most everybody could see how it was with her. Norman was the most favored person in this town. And even as she is the most strange and distant person in Eltopia, there was no denying it. Nancy McGrath had eyes for him. Were they lovers, Sam? Even if you hate the woman, who could blame your father if he wanted to nail some of that."

I let this sink in, still hoping to find a motive for her being up here. "Well, then. A lover's spat. They argued. Or maybe—who knows—people enjoy sex in all manner of ways. And places." I was thinking of Mercedes. "Did it get out of hand? And if he fell, did he reach for her?'

Reuben turned his back to me and walked to the far side of the room. He raised his hands and placed them on the wall.

"What?"

He drew in a deep breath and let it out, then turned back to me.

"He was leaving. Norman was. He told me a week before he died what his plan was."

"Leaving? For where?"

The diamonds were back in Reuben's eyes. "To find you."

I stiffened. "He told you that?"

Reuben nodded. "Your father had been acting strange before he died. Full of regret. I mean, he always had some regret. He even told me that. He said, 'I've made a mess of my life.' He kept talking about how things might have been different."

"But...he had you, Reuben."

He nodded. "But he didn't have you."

Even in the stuffy, breathless heat of the wheat elevator, I felt a chill at my neck. "A spat then. My father told Nancy McGrath and she confronted him. Up here. They argued and she pushed him. Sounds like a scene from Perry Mason."

"But it fits. And as he felt himself falling, he reached for her. And clawed her arm."

For all the years I hated my father, I now felt a new, deeper depth of pain. He was coming, at last, to find me. And he died for it.

"It all looks good on paper, Sam. But proving it is another thing."

We took the lift back down, together this time, and stood staring at the place on the dusty floor where Norman Witt landed. "We may never know," I said. We left the warehouse and Reuben locked the sliding door.

"And then again, we might," he said, walking toward the empty boxcar.

"What day is it?"

"Thursday."

"Train gets me out of here tomorrow."

Reuben shook his head. "You have to stay till next Tuesday."

"I can't."

"Why?"

He had me. Why indeed? "Look, my father is dead, Reuben. Nothing will bring him back. My staying won't do it."

The tall, lean Indian just glared at me, his eyes shining in the dark. "Do me a favor, Sam."

"What?"

"Take that bandage off your eye. It's time. You look like a sympathy case."

I had forgotten it was there, so I ripped it off. "I'm leaving tomorrow," I said.

Reuben had already disappeared into the night, but his parting words came back at me through the dark. "No you're not."

"I can make you breakfast," my wife said. She was out of the shower and she smelled of her shampoo. "We still have three hours. I couldn't sleep either."

"Maybe toast and an egg," I said.

"You're thinking, aren't you Sam?"

I nodded. It was a solemn nod, but she understood that. She knew me too well. And yet, I wondered sometimes if she knew the all of me. I know we were as close as two married people could be, but my drifts into the past were a thing that even I did not fully understand.

"Let's wait an hour before breakfast. Is that okay? I'll come get some coffee though."

"You stay put. I'll bring it to you."

And so she did.

Once gone, I was overcome with memory, so strong that I found myself crying. I had been cheated. I had cheated myself. My years of hating my father had been orchestrated by a litany of lies, poured from the hearts and minds of haters. I had never been a religious man. Not until I met Reuben Flett, the contradiction to nearly everything. The wooden cross around his neck was his most cherished possession, because, he told me, *it solidifies my being here. The Scriptures are not fairy tales, and Satan is the epitome of every bad thing that happens to us. Read Peter.* He said this with such love, that it almost seemed like someone holy was talking. And it was this that had suddenly moved me to tears, because it became clear to me long ago, after visiting Eltopia that Satan had visited Marion Witt in the sanctuary of her dreary kitchen and left his mark on her bitter, hateful heart.

I let myself cry for a time, my face away from the door, in case my wife returned. It was not a matter of shame; we had cried together already over the telegram. But no, this was a personal cry, of the deepest grief. I remember crying like that once before, when my wife was stricken, suddenly, with a case of sharp abdominal pain. Without warning, she was instantly prostrate on the floor. Bent over, I took her to the car and drove her the several blocks to the neighborhood hospital. She was in such pain, and from a cause neither of us knew, so much that I feared it would be her immediate death. As they wheeled her into the examination room, I followed and sat on the floor, holding myself, and watching this dear woman who I worshiped, wrapped in unexplained pain, and I in total fear of losing her. I had never prayed, and cried so hard in my life.

It was diagnosed as diverticulitis and it would take several days before she recovered. Never in my life had I loved my wife more than at that moment when I thought I might lose her. We'd had such a wonderful beginning, and after twenty years together I was not ready to say goodbye.

Walking back to the cabin, I was surprised to see a light on in Nancy McGrath's window. I edged through the dark shadows of the trees, standing at a distance, the light bright. I could see the far wall where a picture hung, and moving to my right, at an angle I saw a bureau. It was her bedroom. I moved closer and stood under the branches of a willow, waiting for I knew not what. Was she already in bed? Reading, maybe?

I was just about to leave and go to my own bed when I saw her enter the room. She was still dressed in the same clothes that she'd worn when we had eaten supper together. I wanted to see the scratches on her arm again, so I crept closer, to within six feet of the window. I was well concealed, and though I had already seen her arm, I wanted to know if she gave them any special attention once her long sleeves were removed. Would she rub them? Would she apply ointment or cream to them? But suddenly, I lost all interest in her arm, as in a few short pulls on her snap buttons, the blouse came off, and there she stood in her bra. I waited, feeling a rush of desire.

Next she bent down and unbuttoned her jeans, kicking them off, and so there she stood, as clear as if I was in the room with her, Nancy McGrath in her panties and bra. My throat tightened. She looked out the window into the darkness and I half expected her to see me, or to simply pull the shade, but she didn't. Her arm and her scratches were getting no attention, but with a simple backward reach behind her, the bra fell and there, displayed for my unexpected pleasure, her milky white breasts. They were not large, like Mercedes', or dainty, like Ashley's. Nancy McGrath's breasts fell into the category of tits—firm and pointy, with brown, erect nipples.

I was in pain now. I was so enthralled with watching her rub away the marks that her bra left, I didn't realize that she had removed her panties too, revealing a forest of pubic hair between her partially opened legs. Nancy McGrath, for all her mystery, was one gorgeous woman. And I was getting a show. She turned, and I watched the wiggle of her ass as she crossed the room, and then, *bonk*, off went the light.

The first trickle of sweat fell from my brow. I stood for a long time in that dark yard, trying to decide if this had accidentally been my lucky night, or if she knew I was there and was setting the stage for bigger things to come. Reluctantly, I slunk back to the cabin like a guilty egg-eating dog. It was sweltering inside but it didn't matter, it would be hours before I could even entertain the idea of sleep. It had been too much of a day. It had been a lifetime inside of a day. I opened the window and left the door wide in hopes of getting a cross draft, but the breeze was still too warm to give off any relief. Mental relief was not there either. Was I on the tipping end of a preposterous lie, or was the real lie the one I had been force-fed by my mother? Who was telling the truth? Here was a town where virtually everyone loved Norman Witt. Yet in Cincinnati, my mother could not mention my father's name without spitting. She could not even read his letters from the war.

...my men assisted the villagers in a burial exercise for two young girls and an old man killed in a freak shelling by a German artillery piece...

The spot where Norman had hit the plank floor in the warehouse circled my mind like a lingering, ugly imprint. It was a signet; as official as a stamp clarifying his death, and for the first time in my life, I found my chest battling despondency over his death, as if I had swallowed a bitter potion.

I forced myself to remember the man who opened the door in our tenement hovel the day he returned from the war, but I could not do it. He appeared only as a shadow in uniform, nothing more. All I could see now was that small pile of stones that marked where his ashes were buried. Reuben Flett had laid a curse at my feet. He, in one day, had managed to twist my history into such a knot, I wondered how it might ever be untangled. If I needed details of who this stranger was, I would have to go back to the schoolhouse and look deeply into the baseball photographs honoring him.

The curtains showed a slight ripple and a moment later I could feel the waited-for breeze. I thought about *A Moveable Feast*, and wondered again about the note inside, and Norman's intention of giving it to me. Was he going to bring it with him when he came, as Reuben said he was planning to do? Or would he send it in the mail ahead of his arrival, as a warning perhaps, or peace offering of some sort?

I moved from the chair to the cot, trying and failing to put meaning to all this confusion. Norman had been dead a little over a week. Reuben had done his body snatching and his investigation and ultimate cremation so quickly it seemed nearly impossible to have been achieved. What if he had done none of it? What if this crazy Indian had just accepted it all and grieved in silence like the rest of Eltopia? Surely I would still hate my father, and likely would be on the train by now back to Cincinnati.

But he *had* done it. He had done it for two reasons—his love for Norman Witt, and because he smelled a rat.

———

I don't remember laying down on the cot, or what my last thoughts were, but I woke to sun through the open door and a raging thirst. It was still early as I wandered into the yard and finding the garden hose, I turned on the spigot and drank deeply of the cold water, and then let it wash against my face. I looked once again at the pump house, its vine covered solitude at the far back of the yard and remembered watching Nancy McGrath going in and coming out yesterday. And the padlock securing the door. Why would a pump house need such safeguarding?

Against my earlier declaration of never eating at the cafe again, I realized it was that or starve. Unless Nancy McGrath decided to invite me in for breakfast, but she wouldn't, because her blue station wagon was already gone. After what I saw of her last night through her window, I wasn't sure I could face her so soon anyway, not with this new image of her nakedness imprinted on my mind.

Sitting in my study now, listening to my wife fiddling around in the kitchen with the toaster, the picture of a naked Nancy McGrath remains, as if a framed portrait in the museum of memory. But that is not the only mental picture I have of her, all these years later. Pictures far more horrible than that. So on that day, in Eltopia, I decided to steel myself for another breakfast at the cafe, and resist any hateful stares from the locals. Even now, it was plainly clear that they did not know what I knew. No one knew. Just Reuben and myself. But then, as I passed by the schoolhouse again, the words of Shim Harden came back to me—*I know something I doubt even Reuben knows.* What possibly could that be? I was tempted to go and ask him, but decided, like he had said, *It can wait.* He had also said, *Trust no one.* That was good armor against the unknowing hostility of the townsfolk.

Tami the pool player was sitting at a booth when I entered the cafe. She was sitting alone with a book in front of her. Looking up, she nodded at me with a smile on her face. I nodded back in reply. Her expression was so welcoming I took a bold step toward her and she motioned for me to sit down, so I scooted into the booth and sat facing her. She was prettier than I remembered, some of the hardness was gone, a ball cap pulled over a ponytail and a faded snap-button cowboy shirt. The shirt was open just far enough to reveal some tanned cleavage.

"What are you reading?" I asked, the only thing I could think of to say.

She pushed the paperback across the table and I picked it up, mostly just to give pause to my sudden discomfort. *The Collector*, by John Fowles. I raised my eyes and she laughed. "It's pretty twisted. Some dude kidnaps this chick and holds her captive. Have you read it?"

I shook my head.

"So, Sam Witt. You're still here. I confess, I'm a little surprised by that."

I attempted a smile. "Me too," I said. Braving a glance around I saw only two other occupants, sitting at the counter, a pair of young Mexican farm workers engaged in a conversation in their own language. Oline was nowhere to be seen. Looking back at Tami I felt a rush of gratitude for her friendliness. "Do you live in Eltopia?"

"I live with Kevin. And he works for George White Auctioneers. He's a mechanic. I work in the scale house at the warehouse. Wheat harvest is a month away, but I hang around just to have something to do. Getting the dingy office organized."

"You said you didn't have a horse in this race," I said, remembering her words. "How's that going? Who's winning and who's losing?"

Tami slid her book back, tapping the cover with chewed fingernails. "Depends. There's folks like me that don't take sides."

"And there's folks that do?"

"It's a small town, Sam Witt, with a lot of small minds. They float their ideas around because there's nothing else to do here. You're at a disadvantage because you didn't show up fifteen years ago. They shared in Norman's world. So, you showing up after he died didn't win you any friends."

"That's become pretty apparent."

"How'd you get that cut above your eye?"

Instinctively my hand went there. "You want the truth, or a story?"

Tami smiled again. "You don't strike me as a story teller."

"I'm not. I can't even figure out my own story."

"Then I guess you'd have to stick to the truth. And honestly, it's none of my business. That helps keep me neutral."

Suddenly Oline was there, having appeared from the kitchen. "Good morning, Sam," she said. "Going to try breakfast again?" She was holding the coffee pot and unconsciously refilled Tami's cup.

"I'm amending my courage. Ruled by my empty stomach."

"Good," Oline said, a crooked, knowing smile. "I'll give you the hungry man special. Tami, you want anything?"

"Just toast. I ate at home when Kevin ate."

Oline touched my shoulder. "Coffee, Sam?"

The sound of my name, coming from her, was like nothing I had ever heard before. There was a lilt to it, a sincerity that not even Mercedes had been able to deliver. The very sound of Oline's voice drew my gaze back to her blue eyes, and I was instantly sorry for ever having heard my name spoken any other way. Tami noted my reaction and tittered softly.

Oline was gone again to the kitchen. Behind me the door opened and turning I saw Reuben Flett enter. Our eyes met, revealing nothing. He stepped behind the counter, grabbed a cup and poured himself coffee. Then he came and sat next to Tami, facing me. Tami showed no surprise.

"We need to take a drive, Sam," he said, his voice cool.

I shot a glance at Tami but she only grinned.

"Can I eat first?"

———

It was because of this road trip with Reuben, from Eltopia up through the basalt corridors of eastern Washington to Grand Coulee, home of the great Grand Coulee Dam that I became an outcast at the public school I was teaching in. And it was because of this road trip that the teacher's union started taking a scrutinizing look at who I was and how I was teaching history. It was because of this road trip that I gradually moved away from teaching out of a government issued textbook and began finding first person narratives from people who had actually lived it. It began with the journals of Lewis and Clark and of Black Elk. It came from the often outlandish tales of David Crockett and the cross continent journals of Robert Louis Stevenson.

It was the high school state test scores that my students started producing in American history that eventually earned me a job at Whittier High School, a school more interested in supporting high achievement, regardless how you come by it. That I took a floundering baseball team from last place to first place in just two years was an added blessing.

Reuben was delivering a load of seed grain to a cooperative in Grand Coulee, in his rattletrap pickup truck, himself acting as tour guide. Every bend in the road, every curve through the high canyons, held some tale of bygone days, relayed with the assurance of a true believer. As we passed, he spoke of Soap Lake, where the unusual body of water produced actual soapy suds along the shoreline. He laughed as he pointed a finger to the far ridge line where a long ago nudist colony once supposedly operated. There was the incredible, carved out landscape of Dry Falls, where the Great Missoula ice dam had burst, centuries before, sending a cataclysmic rush of water down the Clark Fork and Columbia River, flooding great portions of the eastern state. All this 13,000 years ago, yet Reuben spoke as if he'd been there.

He told of Vanport, a city on the Columbia River that vanished in a day because of a flood on the great river on Memorial Day, 1948. A small city there one day, and gone the next, leaving nearly twenty-thousand people homeless.

"It's the river," Reuben said. "It is the mother of this country. It is the history and the future. When they built the dam, my people also lost an entire town. Flooded. And many hold to those old times with a grudge, knowing they will never get it back. Like the buffalo, they grieve for the salmon, though they are still there. But that is not the entire Indian story, Sam."

My wife brings me my toast on a plate into my study and it shakes me from my reverie.

"Where are you, Sam?" she says.

I touch her hand. It is still soft and warm from her shower. I want to kiss her, but I save most of my kisses for bedtime. I shouldn't, and someday I might regret that.

"I am with Reuben," I said. "He is giving me my first glimpse of the Columbia River."

It takes an imagination to look at the Columbia. As my days there would prove. It is a knife blade that cuts through an entire wilderness, from Canada to the Pacific Ocean, dragging history with it, from early natives to Lewis and Clark, to McKenzie, and to the Astor explorers. There are places where it is narrow and other places where it holds the entire country in itself.

Standing open-mouthed at the dam, Reuben pointed to where Norman fell, injuring his back. And how he was taken by ambulance to Spokane where he was put in traction for days on end. His recovery was only partial, hence his college days, his engineering degree, and finally his teaching career at Eltopia. Hearing it all again still did not make it more believable.

On the drive back, Reuben asked about the scratches on Nancy McGrath's arm. "How old would you say they are? I mean, you've seen them, right."

"I've seen them. Yes. And they still showed fairly raw. They were deeper than I originally thought. Still pretty red."

"A week then? Or are they older?"

"I thought we agreed," I said. "They are as old as...as when Norman fell. Why the questions?"

"Because," he said.

I waited. "Are you going to tell me or not?"

"I ran into Bob Granger this morning. Before I found you at the cafe. Out of curiosity, I asked him about that nasty rooster of his. 'Oh, that one, he said. That damn bird was a royal pain in the ass. But he sure tasted good.' I said, Is that a fact? When was that? Bob did some calculating. 'Three or four weeks ago. Memorial Day, it was.'"

My hand went to my face, as if swiping at a smudge that wasn't there. I glanced at Reuben and he raised a single eyebrow.

"There's a lie hiding in that," I said. "In her story."

"It's falling apart."

Looking out the window as we drove, I saw Nancy McGrath naked again, and the momentary hunger that burned at my loins last night. Had Norman's loins burned too? Had they burned often? Who could blame him? Is it possible that she was so possessed of my father that she would rather see him dead than with anyone else? Even with me?

I asked Reuben the same question I'd asked before. "Was my father getting some of that? You know. Nancy McGrath's wares?"

"Why don't you ask her.?"

"Not likely."

"Why not? I have a feeling that if you played your cards right, she'd tell you." He looked at me and winked. "Might even show you."

It was late afternoon when we got back and so I wandered up the hill towards the cabin, head full of visions. But on the way I heard Shim Harden's hammer going at it again, so I entered the schoolhouse. Shim heard my footsteps and found me standing in the hallway, looking again at the photos of the baseball team, and in particular Norman Witt.

"Still here, heh."

I nodded.

"Have you talked to Reuben Flett?"

Facing him, I nodded. "He's told me some fascinating things about my father." I paused. "But I have a question for you, if you don't mind."

"Fire away."

There was no more time for tact. Shim would either tell me or he wouldn't. "What do you know about Nancy McGrath?"

Removing his cap, Shim rubbed his short cropped hair, then ran a palm across his whiskery chin. "There's a lot to know and little to know. That woman might as well be the mayor, if we had one. She's more like the emperor. She's got her fingers in every pie in Eltopia. And none of it officially. The only official thing is her title of postmaster."

"I'm starting to see that."

Shim put up a cautionary hand. "That's all public knowledge, so there's no disputing it. Still," he raised his hand again, "I'm one of the lucky ones that manages to stay out of her way."

"How far out of the way?" I was feeling bold. "Was my father out of her way too, or was he too close?"

"Hell, Sam, that's a loaded question."

"I know it is. I do. But I'm trying to put some pieces together before I head back to Cincinnati. Anything I can learn about their relationship, if there even was one, would be helpful. Besides, you said once you knew some things that even Reuben didn't know about. If you don't mind, what were they?"

Shim considered, and I wondered if he regretted having ever said that. He tilted his head in the direction down the hall, then turned and I followed him. Through a door marked Custodial Closet, we stepped inside and he closed the door. He motioned to a chair and so I sat, while he perched on a stool. "You're leaving, right?"

"As soon as I can."

"Because what I am about to tell you has to go back to Cincinnati with you. It can't stay here. You understand"

He had me now. "Of course," I said.

"Yes."

"Yes, what?"

"Yes, they had a relationship. After your dad had his second back injury, Nancy took him in. She put him in that cabin and she played Nurse Ratched to him."

"Nurse Ratched?"

"*One Flew Over the Cuckoo's Nest*."

"Oh."

"Nancy pandered to your dad, taking meals out to him and the like. But as he got better, she had him in her house every night for supper. Even if she tried to keep it a secret, in this town, it would have been impossible. She didn't care. She felt she had just won the prize of Eltopia. And in a sense, she had."

"And."

Shim toyed with his fingers for a moment. "Because of the affection this town had for your dad, there grew a bit of unease when looking at that situation."

"In what way?"

"Norman was loved. Nancy McGrath is feared."

I waited.

"It became the hush-hush. Had your dad been bought? And at what price? Because what that woman gets, she owns. Her own father seemed like a quaking pigeon around her some times. He was the postmaster before her."

"What happened to him?"

"Word was, he got a job elsewhere. Colorado or someplace like that. One day he was just gone. He was like her that way. Kept to himself. So when he left, no one around here much cared. She took over his duties and the show just went on."

"Is that why we're sitting in a closed room? Is that what you wanted to tell me?"

"Don't get testy, Sam."

My tone had given me away. "Sorry."

"I'm not a suspicious person. But sometimes circumstances create suspicion. It was this spring. April I think. Norman and Reuben had a game in Connell, so they were gone. I was here, doing what I always do, when I get a kid come and tell me I'm needed in the office. Nothing unusual about that. But when I get there, there she is, standing like the Queen of Sheba, still wearing her postal uniform. 'Mr. Harden', she says, 'my pump has stopped working'. What'd you mean, it quit working? 'I have no water in the house. And when I went to the pump house, the pump was not working.'"

Shim Harden had my full attention now.

"After work I wandered over. When I got there she was standing by the pump house door, fidgeting with her keys. When she saw me, she looked over her shoulder, then put the key in that padlock, and opened it."

"Had you ever been inside there before?" I was feeling a bristling of the hair on my neck.

"Never. And she didn't seem too excited about be being in there then either."

"What did it look like inside?"

"It was dark and I told her there was no way I could fix her pump unless she turned a light on. So she pulled a string and the little room lit up. And that's about the extent of it. A small room, taken up mostly by the well-pump and a reservoir tank. There was a little rack to my left that held paint cans. A few rusty garden watering cans. Just junk. She stood with her back against the other wall, trying to look large. As if she was protecting something. Of course, I pretended not to take notice. I just made like I was tinkering with things."

"What else?"

"Well, like I said, there wasn't much about the room to attract my attention. But there was one thing that struck me funny. And that's where my suspicions came in. At first it was just the way she kept fidgeting around. And I kept asking myself, why so nervous? She was like a cat seeing a rat for the first time."

"What?" I wanted Shim to get to the point.

"Well, when I first saw her standing there, outside, I noticed she was holding a couple of letters. She had them pinched pretty tight in her fingers. Once inside, I asked her where the fuse box was. She was still clutching those letters, but when she leaned and pointed to the far wall to where the fuse box was, I got a glimpse of one of the letters she was holding. All I saw was the name and part of the address. She didn't see me. And in truth, Sam, I don't really know why I even looked. It wasn't any of my business anyway."

"But you looked. Whose name, Shim? Whose name was on the envelope?"

Shim Harden looked me in the face for the first time. "Yours, Sam. It was your name."

Stunned, I half stood, then sat down again. "A letter addressed to me?"

"Had Sam Witt printed right there. I saw it under her thumb. And then the tail end of Cincinnati. The cinnati part."

My throat tightened. "Did she see you looking?"

Shim shook his head. "The pump had just blown a fuse. That was all. She didn't know any better. Those old fuses last dang near a lifetime. But she had a box of spares. Probably been there for ages. They were dusty. So I fixed her pump. Before I had much of a chance to explain, she ushered me out and finally came out herself and locked the door."

There was the proof that my father had indeed written me letters, but before I had a chance to consider the truth of this, Shim Harden had one more thing to say.

"Listen now. Nancy McGrath offered to pay me, but I refused. She thanked me, and then reached out and shook my hand. Sam. It was the same hand that the letters were in. But...they weren't there anymore. And they weren't in her other hand either. They were gone. And even when she walked away, I watched her heading back toward her house. They weren't in her back pocket either. They were still in the pump house, Sam. Somewhere. Your letters were gone."

My skin was definitely crawling now. I sat wordlessly for a full minute, Shim watching me.

"Did you tell this to Norman?"

Shim looked down shamefully. "No, I did not. I thought it odd at the time. But it wasn't until you showed up, harping about having never heard from your pa, well, it all came back."

This time I did stand, but only turned around in the small closet, looking but not seeing all the tools and gadgetry hanging from the walls. I wanted a drink. Something stronger than coffee. I wanted to holler my frustration, but my throat was too tight even for that. Shim watched me patiently, then stood himself, and unexpectedly put his hand on my shoulder.

"I've made it worse, haven't I?"

I shook my head. "No. It's only ever been worse." And then I looked at him. "Reuben needs to know this. I have to tell him. Are you okay with that?" But I didn't wait for an answer. Instead I reached for the doorknob and let myself out. He followed me back to the trophy case before speaking again.

"Sam. If I were you, I'd be careful."

Without turning I said, "Careful with who?"

His voice was quiet and filled with wisdom. "Be careful with the truth."

In the pool hall section of the cafe, they served beer. I barely remember walking down the hill, but when I finally did focus, I had a can of Rainier in front of me, icy sweat beads sliding down the side. Behind me was a game of pool going on, and the crack of the balls felt like gunshots in my head. Truth was, I had never fired a weapon in my life. What I was hearing was the gunfire my father must have heard. My shame was building. Here I was, a damn United States history teacher, and I didn't even know what my own father had faced in the war. There was disgrace in the reality of that, and I was going to let it humiliate me, because I deserved the pain of it.

Freezing. Can barely hold the pencil. Leaning against our foxhole, my hand shaking. You may not be able to read this. Cooper next to me, hardly room for either of us. He's spent. We're taking turns sleeping, if you call it that. We're in the woods somewhere and the fog is so damn thick. Can't see two feet in front of us. It's a matter of listening only. Listening for Jerry's tanks that are rumored close by...

I barely heard Oline come from behind me and take the stool next to me.

"Hello, Sam." It was that voice again.

Sitting in my study now, all these years later, I remember the words of Henry Ottoman. *From the day we first met, it was the way she said my name. Henry. There was a sweetness to it. An ownership that only she had title to. When she was gone, I never wanted anyone to speak my name again. But when she came back to me, the first word she said was, Henry. And I came near to tears just hearing it. My name. Henry. Even though it was too late, it still sounded right.*

And so here, Oline, who I barely knew, seemed to punish me with the sweetness of her voice, and the way she spoke my name. Her brown hair was to her shoulders, her waitress smock across her lap. It carried the faint scent of bacon and coffee. Guiltily, I wondered what her personal scent would be like, maybe after her bath. She was sitting too close to let this line of thinking go further.

"Break time?"

"No, Glenda came in. My shift is over," she said.

With this nice girl sitting next to me, I tried immediately to shift my mind away from Shim Harden and his confession. Here was a much more appealing distraction. I dared a look at her and her blue eyes, like the positive pole of a magnet, drew me deep. My words caught in my throat. This was not Mercedes. This was an angel.

"Are you drowning your sorrows, Sam?"

I forced a laugh. "Something like that, I guess."

She was quiet for a moment. "That probably wasn't the right thing to say."

I shook my head. "No, it was the perfect thing to say. Because it's true."

"Pretty bad?"

What to tell this woman. Someone who loved my father when I hated him, and yet willing to give me the room to stand up to the truth. But what is the truth. Regardless, I had crossed a threshold there was no turning back from.

"I'm learning some things." I had to look straight ahead in order to speak, the beer sitting in front of me, untouched.

"I'm keeping you from your thoughts. I should go."

Before realizing it, I placed my hand on hers. "Please. Stay. You're one of the few friends I have here. If I may call you a friend."

Instead of a yes or no, she said, "Who are your other friends?"

"Well..."

"Look at me, Sam Witt. I want to see your eyes."

It was a command, and though I was a bit startled by it, I turned and gazed at her. "What are you looking for?"

"I'm looking for you. For who you are. You're in there, somewhere, I suppose. In your brooding."

"Am I an open book?"

"You have secrets. That much I can see."

I nodded. "A deep well of them."

"There's a bench down the path. Under a tree. Grab your beer. I think we need to talk."

Oline did not wait for an answer, instead she stood, threw her apron over her shoulder, and headed for the door. So, Rainier in hand, I followed her. She was right, there was a bench under an elm tree, just far enough away to offer privacy, and just near enough to start a wagon load of gossip. She sat and I sat next to her.

"Your friends? Who are they?"

I thought deep on this, considering my life as a whole. "Friends?" I said. "I'm embarrassed to say, you've caught me at a loss. On the face of it, I'm not sure I have any friends. Growing up in the tenements, the people I hung around with could be my friends one day and my enemies the next. It was a rough neighborhood."

Oline said nothing, just listened, expecting me to continue. I stared at her hands, which were resting in her lap. They were worker's hands; gardener hands as I would learn later.

"My hatred towards my father has a place of origin. And I am increasingly more ashamed of that. I'm finding out that one person's truth is different from another's. In fact, I'm finding out that there are haters in this world, and there are lovers. My mother was...*is* a hater. It is a pathetic sight to behold. What's worse? She turned me into one."

Oline put her hands together, as if in prayer, and looked across the field to where sheep were grazing in a pasture. I followed her gaze, waiting for anything she might have to say, but she said nothing. Yet I knew her words would come soon enough, so I went on.

"I have learned more in twenty-four hours from a crazy Indian than I have in my twenty-six years being a victim. In my neighborhood you had to fight for your territory. I never wanted any territory. I just wanted to be left alone. I guess I truly am the proverbial lone wolf. But Reuben put me on my ass without a second thought. How do things like that happen?"

"Oh, Sam," she laughed. "It wasn't Reuben who did that. It was your father. He's the one that taught Reuben to defend himself. Reuben needed that, because he had a tough road too. Just like you. You might call that poetic justice."

It felt good to hear her talk. I wanted to hear more, but she was not taking the bait.

"I teach history to a bunch of at-risk kids. In the inner-city of Cincinnati. They love me. Most of them. Because they feel I am one of them. Some of them are black. Some Latinos. Some poor white kids. But I don't see them by color. Or anything else. I just see them as kids who may always have a tough road ahead. Many of them are fatherless too, just like me. Isn't that how it always works. The hurt helping the hurt."

Finally I was getting tired of hearing my own voice so I stopped.

"I am an orphan, Sam. My parents died in a freak accident. I was five. The whole town was lost."

"Vanport?"

"How did you know about that?"

"Reuben told me. But I didn't know you were there. He didn't tell me that. I'm sorry. Who? How?"

"My aunt and uncle. It's where I live." She pointed in the direction where the canyon rim branched out west of town.

I tried clumsily to calculate her age. Twenty-two. If my numbers were right. Oline was twenty-two.

"We're not that different, Sam. In some ways, at least."

This was a sobering revelation. Could I possibly bear more shame? This time I looked at her without flinching. There was beauty there that I had not seen before. Her face more the soft skin of a child. Yet she was no child. Her eyebrows suddenly evoked a memory. I was fifteen when I saw the black and white movie, *The Country Girl*, with Bing Crosby and William Holden. But it was Grace Kelly that slipped into my teenage fantasies. It was a drama that fit my life; the rage, the drunkenness of my mother. But on the screen was a woman so beautiful she took my breath away. Her eyebrows were the window to her very eyes, and I went back to the theater and watched the movie three more times. All because of Grace Kelly and her eyes and eyebrows. Now, holding my gaze, I saw it all over again, the country girl beauty of a Grace Kelly in this backwater town. I was mesmerized.

"Sam. Can I tell you something?"

I managed a smile. "You have my full attention, lady."

She didn't blush, but it was close. She blinked, looked off at the sheep again. "This isn't what I was going to say. But I think you need to hear this first."

I was warming to this country girl. "What's that?"

She kept her gaze on the pasture. "Making a personal observation, of course. But, you are more handsome today that you were two days ago. You've lost some of that bitterness. It was all over you that first day. But some of that is gone now."

Mercedes used to tell me I was handsome, but it seemed like the regurgitation of words she had spoken to other men she had known. A pat phrase so generic it meant nothing. But there was nothing common about how Oline said it. It felt honest, words so uniquely owned by this young woman, who I guessed was only familiar with truth. And part of that truth was that I had already undergone some kind of transformation. I was not out of the woods with my sadness, but my anger and bitterness, for the time being, needed to be put in storage until I learned more.

"Okay," I said, hoping my tone was appreciative.

Oline stared ahead. "What do you know about sheep, Sam?"

"Ha. Absolutely nothing. I'm a city boy, remember."

"That can be forgiven too."

"Too?"

"What do you know about the Bible?"

Uh oh, I thought. "Well, about the same as sheep. Not much. What's your point?"

She didn't say anything, just sat there, staring at the sheep, so all that was left for me to do was the same, and wait for the other shoe to drop. It was slow in coming, so I finally said, "I'm listening."

"Most everyone on the planet, non-believers included, have heard the story of the lost sheep. I'm guessing you have too."

I nodded, guiltily.

"Do you think you're here by accident, Sam?"

I had no answer for this.

"I'll take that as a no. Because you're not. Life is too big for that kind of thinking. From the little you have told me, about your life, God figured you needed a wake-up call. It's just too bad it came too late."

Two days ago I would have gotten up and walked away. This sort of stuff always made me feel uncomfortable. But I didn't. "So, I'm the prodigal son?"

Oline pointed. "See that lamb over by the fence? The one with the black feet? Ted Darcadus found that little fellow two weeks ago. It was caught in a tar marsh a couple of miles away. Nobody knows where or why it got there. It was too far away from any other pastures."

I looked. "Is that supposed to be me?"

"Sam. I didn't want my parents to die in that flood." She finally turned and looked at me. "For a long time I wished I had died with them. Sometimes, when I wake up, facing the same thing every day, I still wonder why I didn't. I wonder what the point is."

She had silenced me.

"I doubt my parents were perfect. But when you lose them at such a young age, all you remember are their goodness. I don't know what happened to you, Sam. Someday you can tell me everything. If you think it will help. But I do know that on this end of things, Norman Witt loved his son."

Her blue eyes were too much and I looked away.

"And don't I act like I know everything?" Humility rose in her voice.

Head down, and again I said, "I'm listening."

"That's all. I should be going."

I could still feel her eyes on me.

"I can't bring my parents back. And you can't bring your father back. But at least you have a chance at seeing who he really was."

Oline stood and I watched her walk away, down the gravel lane towards where she lived with her aunt and uncle, where a tree-lined, white clapboard house stood beneath the red of the basalt arroyo.

The beer rested on the bench beside me until it lost its chill, but after a while I drank it anyway. Twilight was approaching over the rim rocks and the sheep, somehow sensing this, moved to the shelter of a ramshackle barn for reasons of their own. Yet I stayed, planted to the bench, deep in thought. Oline's words had found their place. Everyone has a story. And mine was not as unique as I had always made it out to be. How pitifully selfish I had become. And I couldn't even blame my mother anymore, because I had the same choices before me that anyone else might have had. A better man than me would have burned with a desire to know the truth behind my father's disappearance. A better man than me would have made this trip ten years ago, and heard the truth from my father's own lips.

And then the face of Nancy McGrath intersected my thoughts like a black shadow, and a thing even deeper than fear stiffened me. *What was in that pump house she so diligently protected?* I wondered. How deep could this thing go? Could the skin found under Norman's fingernails be the skin from Nancy McGrath's arm? Or was Reuben Flett just inventing imaginary evidence to sooth his grief?

In the darkening evening, I shot another glance to the lane where Oline had gone down, she in her peculiar wisdom, and I wondered what she would say about all of this. How much stock would she put in Reuben's theory? This was not something to ask her. It was a question for Reuben. Who in this town could be trusted, and was Oline one of them?

In a corner of my study rests my father's trunk from the cabin. It came back with me to Cincinnati. Inside lies the truth.

"I saw your light on. Can I come in?"

It was Nancy McGrath, standing outside the cabin door. I had not been sleeping. My mind was too cluttered for anything resembling sleep. But this I was not prepared for. Was it too late to feign sleep? Clearly it was.

"Come in," I said, without enthusiasm.

The first thing I saw was her wet hair and I judged she had just gotten out of the shower. She had on a loose-fitting, long-sleeved sweater and a pair of gray sweatpants, and she showed no hesitation in coming in. Since I was sitting on the cot, she made straight for the chair, the scent of floral soap coming in with her.

"I was a little surprised you were still here," she said, leveling a quizzical look. "You sounded like you were anxious to be gone."

I tried to be ingenious. "Must be the country air. We don't get things like this in Cincinnati."

She wasn't humored. "I imagine you've found Reuben Flett by now. Or he has found you."

I gave her a slow nod.

She sighed. "Reuben, as you have probably heard by now, was a doting orphan who followed your father everywhere. Something like a stray dog. I'm sure he would have you believe they were close."

My hackles were raising.

"But, that's neither here nor there. I'm sure you're smarter than to believe his imaginings."

A protest was building in me, but I resisted. It was beginning to take on a he-said, she-said case, and if I was playing the wise juryman, I would listen rather than speak. Fortunately she changed the subject.

"Actually. When I saw your light I wondered if you had eaten. I did.

But there's leftovers. I could make you a roast beef sandwich."

"I already ate," I lied. But instantly I regretted saying that. A thought had struck me, so I added, "But a sandwich does sound good."

Nancy McGrath stood, and crossing the short distance to my cot, reached out her hand. Confused, I hesitated, but she kept her hand out until I finally took it in mine. She then lifted me from my perch and led me to the back door of her house, like a mother leading a child, the cabin door left wide open. It was as awkward and confusing as having both our hands in the cookie dough that first night.

Inside, I sat at the kitchen table and watched her prepare my sandwich as I had done before. But my peripheral was looking for something else—a key rack. I had that pump house on my mind and I was hoping I might see a holder of some kind where often-used keys might be hanging. I let my eyes cover every wall and corner but I saw nothing. In fact, there wasn't much of anything hanging from the walls. Funny I hadn't noticed that before. There were no quaint kitchen type pictures anywhere to add feeling to the place. Not even a plant or flower. The flowers she had on the table the first night had vanished. I turned casually in my chair, scanning the wall behind me, but they were bare as well. Just a sea of kitchen-white. For whatever reason, I was bothered by this. Was this woman completely lacking in imagination? And how could my father have endured such a drab environment. Even in the cabin there hung a Remington print of an Indian holding up the skull of a buffalo over his head. I doubted it was hung there by Nancy McGrath.

Furthermore, with the exception of peering into her bedroom last night, this was the only room I had ever been in, this suddenly dreary kitchen. Even getting here I was led down that same dark hallway, with doors closed on either side. And to my shame, last night, I wasn't looking at the walls of her bedroom. I was looking at her—her forty-something beauty the only decoration I saw.

The sandwich was made and placed in front of me on a plate, but I was a long ways away from desiring even a crumb of it. I felt suddenly as if I was back with Mercedes and her constant captaining of every situation. Nancy McGrath wanted me here for some reason she hadn't revealed yet, but I was feeling the need to fortify myself against whatever it was. She sat across from me, waiting expectantly for me to yield to her will. But what was her will?

"Sam," she said, her voice like the cooing of a pigeon. "What draws you back to Cincinnati so soon? You just got here."

I instantly hated her. Not only was her voice counterfeit, her words were the poison I had been waiting for. I was pretty sure now that she had seen me in the darkening yard last night, perhaps waiting for hours for me to show myself, so as to put on her display of nakedness for my benefit. For what she hoped would be her eventual benefit. It was clear now what she wanted—she wanted me. I looked at her, and there was power in that face, and I felt myself shrinking. How far would she take me before there was no turning back? Before the web was too tangled for escape. Yes, it was Mercedes all over again, the command and the control. With one big exception, Mercedes had not killed my father.

There, I had said it. I had said it in my mind anyway. I had been shown too much to doubt it now. I was seated at the table of a murderer. And I wondered, with a degree of fright, if she was seeing Norman and not me. Was she hoping to resurrect the man she thought she could possess, but when she realized she couldn't, she gave him a push? But then, just like Lazarus—another Bible story I'd heard—her lover was back, alive and well. I needed no more convincing. Nancy McGrath was mad.

She put her hand out across the table, expecting me to take it, the sandwich, by now, forgotten by both of us. My hands remained in my lap.

"Do you have someone waiting for you?" she asked. "In Cincinnati?"

My mind went to Ashley first, then to Mercedes. I feared my expression was saying *no*, so I dropped my eyes. Was this supposed to be her idea of pursuit, this clumsy, insult to romance? And then, as if remembering my part in a bizarre play, a line from a James Wright poem I had been forced to memorize in college, came creeping back into my head. *I pity myself, because a man is dead*, and an unforeseen rage came over me.

"Yes, in fact. We're to be married next month," my voice terse.

Nancy McGrath did not flinch, but I could see her temples begin to flush. Her head moved slightly, and she brushed back a strand of blond hair that didn't need straightening. "Seems I lose all my men to Cincinnati," she said, in a voice meant for her hearing only. She appeared to be lost all of a sudden, a change passing so quickly, like a cloud across the moon, and I felt my nerves tighten. I sensed her eyes were not seeing me anymore, but seeing straight through me.

Then, as suddenly as it had come, it left, and she smiled. "Sam, you haven't touched your sandwich."

I looked at the plate. "You're right," I said. "I guess I wasn't as hungry as I thought."

She was up then, and with a surprising efficiency, produced a roll of waxed paper, and with a few quick gestures, had my sandwich wrapped up. "You can eat it later. It'll be good for breakfast." She handed it to me with an abruptness which seemed to signal that I had spoiled her evening. And then she added, "It'll be better than anything you'll get at that cafe."

I left with my sandwich, surprised she didn't put up a better fight. It was plain to see where her intentions had been when she invaded the cabin. But her plan went sour when I lied about getting married. Even at that, I expected her to brush that aside as a mere gnat. Nancy McGrath, for all I had heard, always got what she wanted. But then, my father's ashes were just over the far hill in a rim rock cove, proving that theory false.

Henry Ottoman and I became friends when he joined the staff of Wittier High School in 1984, and by 1988 he was that broken man, whose wife had left him. Even in the middle of his trials, he was able to jokingly be thankful for the fact he taught math and algebra. *Numbers and formulas don't change, Sam. So I don't have to put much thought into teaching. It's all the same every day and so it doesn't require a lot of energy on my part.* It was not uncommon for Henry and me to have lunch together in my classroom. He asked a lot of questions about baseball, but invariably it led to his personal life and the mess that had been caused by it.

"Life's never perfect," I told him, sharing various parts of my own.

Henry was a good listener. His wife had been gone for six months by that time. "I know what I do every night in my little house. It's always the same. Just like an algebraic equation. Perfect balance. Maybe that's what caused Susan to leave me. I was too regular. Too predictable. She could always count on me and she was sick of counting on me. She wanted an adventure, and she used her garden nursery as a catalyst."

I too was a good listener, so I let him theorize.

"Sometimes, Sam, I even bore myself."

And there it was, I thought, looking back on 1965 and Eltopia. My place in the universe, leading up to that dangerous summer, was worth less than a wooden nickel. Oline's words, sitting on the bench, had sent me into a swamp of awakening. Who the hell was I? And who, based on my milquetoast attitude, was I ever going to become. I could live my life on the south side of pity, or I could be the lost sheep that came home. Even in the middle of solving the death of my father, I was hedging my bets.

Obviously it wasn't Henry's words that inspired me to do what I did next, as I didn't even know him yet, rather it was Oline's words. Or, if not her words exactly, it was the clear and visible truth spoken through her expression, that I was scarcely worth the ink printed on my birth certificate. In her eyes, what she hoped to see was the son of Norman Witt, not the son of Marion Witt. Those blue eyes said one thing, clear as river water—*Do you want to find out what happened to your father, or don't you?*

At that point in my life, in early summer, my understanding of sin was pretty shallow. But even so, I knew what I was about to do was a sin, but it also had a motive. For one night only, I would play the devil's advocate, for whatever it might benefit me in getting to the bottom of things. I was willing to go the distance, if required, and if it was my downfall, I would at least be in the good company of my father.

Moving back across the lawn, I knocked on Nancy McGrath's door. I waited, listening for her footfalls, expecting her to ask who it was, but she didn't, instead she said, "Is that you, Sam?"

"Yes. It's me."

I had been in the cabin maybe fifteen minutes, but when she opened the door she was already in her night robe. "Did you forget something?" She faked a degree of modesty. "Excuse the way I look. I was about to get in the shower."

My eyes panned her. "Not exactly," I said. "I was thirsty. I was wondering if I could trouble you for a beer. It's pretty warm in the cabin. It will go good with my sandwich. That is if you don't mind me asking."

"Come in, Sam." She stepped back and allowed me to pass.

I moved down the familiar dark hallway into the kitchen. Nothing had changed. Even the chair I had been sitting in hadn't been pushed in. Taking the bold initiative, I sat down in it. Nancy McGrath showed no surprise, rather opened the refrigerator and leaned in to retrieve a beer. When she bent over the fold of her bath robe opened, just enough to expose one of her breasts. She held that pose long enough for me to know it was intentional. Instead of one beer, she set two Rainiers on the table.

"Do I look a fright?" she asked.

This was going easier than I expected. "Not at all. You look the same as when I just left."

"I mean the getup. Robe and all."

"It's your house. You can dress however you want."

She sat down across from me and pushed one beer towards me. "Have one here, Sam. You can take another one with you. Whenever you decide to leave."

Nancy McGrath was putting up an excellent impersonation of Mercedes Belfour. She was playing her cards face-up.

Opening my beer, I took a drink. It tasted good and I congratulated myself on my ploy in getting inside. All systems forward. "To be honest, I was feeling a bit lonesome. You know. Thinking about my fiancé and all. I've never been away from her before."

She said nothing, but her eyes seemed fixed on my face.

"I'm sorry. My father's only been gone, what, a week and a half.

You're probably lonesome too." For having never taken an acting class in my life, I felt I was holding my own.

Her eyes kept boring into me. "Yes, Sam. I do get very lonesome," she said, her voice husky and low. "Your father was a good friend to me. And now he's gone. I mean, gone from me. I suppose that seems selfish, spoken to someone who never got to know him."

Returning her gaze, I said, "One doesn't miss what they never had. But you had him, so...I understand why you're lonely." I watched her closely, trying to notice anything strange in her behavior. She was rubbing the top of one of her thumbnails with her other thumb, back and forth. Was it a habit, or was it just a means of masking the shakiness I had seen on other occasions?

"Norman...your father, was a tender man. But a haunted man. He had a hard time understanding the cruelties of life."

This was a twist. A survivor of the war, not able to understand the cruelties of life. "What do you mean?"

Nancy McGrath put her hand on the table, hoping, I assumed, that I would reach out and take it. Was it an invitation? Taking the risk, I reached out and put my hand over hers. Her skin was softer than I expected, for a letter handler, but it was warm. And yet, I noticed a faint energy running thought her hand, even up her arm, as if my touch was either causing it, or helping control it.

"Would I be out of place, Sam Witt, if...if I told you I loved your father?"

"I've heard that from a lot of people since I got here. That he was loved."

She shook her head. "No!" It was nearly a shout. But she caught herself. "No, it was not like the rest of these people. What did they know about him anyway? Did that Indian ever put Norman to bed when he hurt his back? Or any of the rest of the gossips in this town. They only knew what they saw. I knew what..."

Suddenly Nancy McGrath stopped. As suddenly as her mood had changed earlier when the business of Cincinnati came up. Yet her eyes widened slightly, still trained on me, or through me. I waited for what was to come next. I didn't have to wait long.

"Make love to me, Sam. I need you to make love to me." She stood then, and opening her robe, revealed herself completely. "No one will know. Your fiancé will never know. Before you leave, Sam." She took a step toward me, and then another and so I stood. Would this lead to my answer?

Nancy McGrath put her hand on my face, and having decided to go the distance, I reached out and took one of her breasts in my hand. In an instant she was kissing me. Savagely. And then she was pulling me out of the kitchen and towards the hallway to her bedroom. Halfway there I pushed her against the wall and kissed her back, letting my hands pull the robe off her shoulders. And then I leaned in hard against her. The corridor was dark but I could feel her breath on my neck, the panting of a forest creature.

Putting my mouth close to her ear, I whispered. "Did my father love you like this?"

It was like a douching of cold water. Her head snapped up, and with both hands pushed me hard against the other wall. She raised her hand to slap me, but caught herself. "No!" It was that near shout again. "No, no, no."

Light from her bedroom was brightening the hallway now and I could see her better. I moved towards her, and taking a chance, put my hands softly on her face. She didn't resist. I kissed her forehead.

"He didn't love me." She shook her head. "If he loved me he wouldn't have left me."

"But he didn't leave you."

"Oh, he was going to. He was going back to Cincinnati." She spat the word as if it was profane. "Going to see *you*." She suddenly realized that I was the very reason for him leaving, and she abruptly pushed me away again. "You, Sam. Norman loved you more than he loved me."

I staggered. "What happened?"

"What do you mean, what happened? He fell at the warehouse and died." She moved closer again. Taking my hands, she moved them back to her breasts. "Please, Sam. For me. I won't tell."

Not the years. Not even the quietness of my study. Or the rain on the window. Nothing can erase what happened that night. I was sincerely hoping to extract a confession from Nancy McGrath, and I gave myself over to the last full measure. There can be no denying the fact that lust did take over and it became a duel mission, one that returned empty; the other etching a memory of the deepest regret into the story of that summer. Yet even regret can come wrapped in a tantalizing package, and Nancy McGrath was all of that. Still, for all my efforts, no confession came from it.

Only two more times would I ever see her again. And those times were drawing near.

Waking in the middle of the night and fumbling for my clothes, I took a long, regretful gaze at this woman, both lonely and passionate, yet possibly capable of murder. My stomach was in a state of recoil, knowing I had just had sex with the woman who may have been my father's lover. Passing through the kitchen, I saw the two beers still setting on the table. As a sudden afterthought, and with an ear cocked for any sound from the bedroom, I quietly started pulling out drawers, hoping to find the key to the pump house. But the only light was the moon through the window, and I couldn't risk turning on a light.

So, my search was short-lived and I found nothing. Until. Opening a drawer on the furthest end of the counter, where the light was poor, I reached in, careful not to grab hold of a sharp knife. I felt my fingers wrapping around something cold and metallic. I lifted it out and was so shocked I nearly dropped it. A live snake couldn't have been more alarming. It was a pistol. In my life I had never held a weapon like this before. Even in the tenements, it was our fists and cunning that did the work for us. But here, heavy in my hand, was a coal black handgun. I felt myself bristle under its weight.

What was Nancy McGrath doing with a big pistol like this? Was it part of a safety measure as postmistress? If so, why wasn't it in her blue station wagon where harm was more likely to come? Or was it simply a sleeping aid for living alone? Who knew what danger might be lurking outside her door. Listening for any sound from her bedroom, I moved to the moonlight and stared at it. It was not new, yet not a relic either. I knew next to nothing about pistols, and I had never held one, but I knew exactly what it was. I hadn't been delinquent in my research when teaching history. This pistol I recognized by its wartime fame—a 1911 Colt .45, Army issue. It chilled me, and so I returned it to the drawer and left the house.

In the cabin's small shower, I tried to wash away the shame of what I had just done. Standing under the spray for a long time, I was able to retrace any words that may have slipped from Nancy McGrath's mouth that could have lent itself to the mystery, and why I was there. But not once did she call out the name of my father by mistake in her ecstasy. So, my efforts, for the most part, were lost, save what seemed that we, as animals, needed. But now I was afraid. What if my deeds got out? Would Reuben think I'd betrayed him? And Oline, what about her?

Dressed, I followed a pink sliver of dawn to the top of the hill where the little cemetery was said to be. I found it, a haven for weeds and dead souls, surrounded by a rusty wire fence. I entered where the fence had fallen and walked towards the back where the earth had been freshly turned and a well-honed cross, likely the work of Shim Harden, planted in front of the mound. Here is where one person said Norman Witt was buried and another person said he wasn't. Inwardly I tried to gauge the difference in their stories. Only one was telling the truth.

My thoughts were interrupted by the sound of Nancy McGrath's blue station wagon revving up. Turning and looking down at her house from this higher perch, I felt I was viewing things from a completely different perspective. Everything seemed uniform, as if in a sketch of Winnie the Pooh's Hundred Acre Wood. Trees, the cabin, her tidy, clapboard house, the removed cubicle that served as the post office, and finally the mysterious pump house. The whole of it appeared surreal and for a brief foolish moment I wondered if I was Christopher Robin, and I had stumbled into something too big for me to comprehend. Too big to solve. I had come here to get away from Mercedes Belfour and maybe to collect my hated father's belongings. Yet now I was gazing down at a fairyland. Perhaps a dark one. Not Peter the Rabbit, rather something much darker, something closer to the Brothers Grimm.

Nancy McGrath was going somewhere and I presumed it was duty related. I knew she made frequent trips to Ritzville, but also south into Pasco. I watched as she carried a small box of what looked like letters to the station wagon where she put them in the back seat. But then I saw her pause, hands on hips, eyes fixed in the direction of the cabin. There was an elm tree close to where I was standing, so I moved and stood behind it. After another moment, I saw her walking to the cabin. The door was on the far side of me, but I guessed she entered, hoping to find me there, because after a moment I saw her reappear and scan the surrounding roads and fields, looking for me. Not finding me, she walked back to the car, backed out of the dirt driveway, and drove away. At the main road I saw her turn left, which meant she was going to Ritzville. Here was my chance.

Forty years gives a man plenty of time to reshape what happened in the next eighteen hours, to give anecdotes and metaphors to the events that followed, perhaps to give better clarity to a man's soul. Or to help unburden it. It took me years to appreciate poetry, but once I was able to relate to it, and not try to find the poet's deeper meaning, rather put my own meaning to it, I became an avid appreciator of it. It was Robert Lowell that grabbed me in my earliest ventures into the art, and I found in his poem, *Epilogue*, the explanation I needed—*Those blessed structures, plot and rhyme / why are they no help to me now / I want to make / something imagined, not recalled?* Macbeth entered in too.

What did I know about women? My youthful love for Ashley was a crush based on familiarity. We walked the same sad tenement streets together and shared the same hard knocks of missing or alcoholic parents. We found a simplicity in our affection for each other, in an age where there was no other thing approaching simplicity. We knew each other's story and it made us strong. But fiction is bred from reality. Nothing in Macbeth, nor even a *Travis McGee* mystery could prepare me for the numbing blow of the coming hours. The events would stand on their own, like the skeletons they would become.

Seeing Nancy McGrath's station wagon reach the blacktop highway, I marched down the hill and went directly to her back door, the same one I'd exited from only hours before. It was locked, as I expected it would be. There was another door around the corner, obviously little used, as weeds had grown up through cracks in the sidewalk, and a massive spider's web hung from the screen door, spider intact. I brushed it away, opened the screen door and tried the knob. The knob was locked but the door pushed open.

What was I doing? Turning slowly I scanned the fields and gravel roads at my back. I could see the school and further down the hill, the cafe. Even the wheat warehouse was visible, sliding door open, but not Reuben, nor any other soul stirred. For the first time I realized how muggy the air had become, and looking further on, towards where my father's ashes were buried, I saw a sinister bank of dark clouds forming in the distance. I turned back to the door. The minute I walked into that house, I would be committing a crime. It wasn't exactly *breaking* and entering, it was just illegal entrance. Didn't matter. They were both against the law.

I stepped inside.

Here was a part of the house I had never seen, a part where doors had been closed. A shock of fear struck me suddenly that a guard dog might be kenneled somewhere in one of the rooms, and I paused in the dark room and listened for anything that sounded like a growl. Nothing. Relaxing, I stepped out from the clammy, airless vestibule into what must have been the living room, but it was clearly unused. The heavy curtains were drawn, with only a crease of sunlight coming through at the top of the windows.

An ottoman nearly tripped me up, and I had to catch myself, sending up a puff of dust into my nose. The furniture was lifeless, a chair and a sofa shoved against different walls with a coffee table so dusty I could have written a message on it. This was not a living room; it was a dead room. I could only wonder why it was neglected. It only added to the peculiarity of Nancy McGrath. I felt safe in assuming that my father had never been in this room.

Crossing to a door, I opened it slowly, still thinking of a dog hiding inside, only to find it darker yet. My palm searched the wall for a light switch and finding it, flipped it up. The ceiling bulb took a long time to engage and when it finally did, the bulb was so dirty it scarcely put off any light. But it didn't matter, because the room was empty, save for an old army cot with a drab army blanket thrown over it, concealing a small mound of something beneath it, likely more blankets and pillows.

A last door, when opened, found me back into the hallway that led to the kitchen and welcome sunlight through the windows, where I immediately had a sneezing fit because of the dust. Here everything was polished and clean, as if I had just passed through Alice's looking glass from a dirty rabbit's hole. Quickly, I started in my search in earnest again for the key to the pump house. Still, I needed to make sure I left everything as I had found it, so my search became more with my eyes than with my hands. But after looking deeply into every drawer and cupboard, I found nothing that looked like a key.

Back into the bedroom, the crime scene of last night's sin, I found the bed neatly made up, as if not even she had slept there. I checked her closet, finding a scant few dresses and shoes. It was but a microcosm of what Mercedes closets looked like. The chest of drawers held mostly a mound of panties and several bras, which I delicately moved to search underneath. The next was folded blouses and finally folded blue jeans. But no key.

But what I had missed the night before was a sturdy hook screwed into the ceiling toward the window where a potted plant hung, the dangling vines, green and happy, spilling over the side of the pot. It wasn't hard to understand why I'd missed it, considering I was following a naked woman into the room, and that Nancy McGrath immediately turned off the light when we entered. I doubted a key would be hidden in the pot, and there was no way to find out without standing on the bed, which seemed pointless.

Still, standing, glaring at the hanging plant, just far enough out of reach, I wondered what Sherlock Holmes would say—*There is nothing more deceptive than an obvious fact.* Looking around for a foot stool and finding none, I climbed onto the very bed that harbored my sin of hours before. Leaning out, legs wobbling, I let my fingers play around in the soil, poking and searching, nearly falling twice, but without any success. I thought about removing the pot from the big hook, but decided against it. Enough was enough. But getting down from the bed I saw I had left dusty footprints on the bedspread. I carefully swept them away and tidied the bedding, but then I realized I had likely left footprints in the living room when I'd walked through the dirty floor. It was too late to worry about that. By the looks of it she never went in there anyway. I checked the rest of the bedroom and kitchen for telltale tracks but found none.

My search was over, and disappointed as I was, I was relieved to be shed of the place.

Reuben Flett was at the warehouse, sweeping the concrete floor that needed no sweeping. I told him everything. It was time I trusted him fully. Reuben was a handsome man, his braids woven tightly, a ball cap and neckerchief as much a part of him as his gleaming, dark eyes. And it was those eyes, both mocking and smiling, that nailed me to my shame when I revealed what I had committed myself to the night before. I held nothing back and, outside of a few incredulous shakes of his head at my audacity, he listened.

After I told him about Shim Harden's revelation, I said, "I want inside that pump house."

Reuben took a few more meaningless pushes with the broom, the turning of his mind like the gears of a machine. "So. What do you propose?"

I shrugged. "You're the body snatcher. I was hoping you'd have an idea."

"What kind of lock is on the door?"

"A standard padlock."

He disappeared into the shadows, replacing the broom to its place. For a long minute he stood in the dark, thinking. When he emerged from the darkness, there was a shine to his face that told me he wasn't taking this thing lightly. He crossed his arms over his chest.
"There's man's laws and there's God's laws."

I waited.

"If we break into Nancy McGrath's pump house, we are liable for unlawful entry. She could have us arrested."

At that time in my life I had no idea what God's laws might be.

"King David and his men once ate five loaves of the Holy sacraments in Nob. His men were hungry and the sacred bread was all there was to eat. He told the priest, Ahinelech, that it was told him by God."

It was my turn to look incredulous. "Okay?"

"It appeared that God had given King David a pass to His own rules. The point being, it was meant for good."

"Okay," I said again, trying to follow where Reuben was taking this.

"What exactly do you think you'll find in there? Fair question."

"Fair answer? I don't know. I just know something is in there that maybe shouldn't be. Not just what Shim saw. Or felt he saw. But I watched her myself. She went out there with a bag and come back with nothing. That was day before yesterday."

"Feeding a pet rat."

"Maybe. Tell me I'm crazy and I'll drop the whole thing."

Reuben shook his head. "I don't know how this would tie into Norman's death. But I think she's lying about everything. I think she is guilty of murder. As for the pump house. There's ways to get in there, I suppose. But it isn't something we can do in broad daylight."

"When, then?"

Reuben looked at me. "Midnight."

"It's dark back there."

"I'll bring a flashlight and a screwdriver. And..." He closed his eyes, imagining the whole thing. 'We'll know in the first ten seconds if it's something we can open."

My own mind was swimming, now that Reuben was onboard. "But...what does this have to do with eating five loaves of bread."

He shook his head. "I thought you were a teacher. Haven't you ever opened a book?"

"I haven't opened the Bible, if that's what you mean."

"Mores the pity. That's where all the answers are."

"I feel a sermon coming on. I already got one from Oline."

He raised an eyebrow. "There's a lot of orphans in this town. You're not the only one."

The pain in his words were clear, and they stung.

"Ahinelech asked King David if his men had been with any women. He said they had not. It was the only way the priest would give the holy bread to David." There was that dark stare again, an arrow that found its mark. "I know someone who has."

"Reuben. It was a story."

The arrow was still there. "Try not to show your ignorance, Sam Witt. It's not helpful."

Back in the cabin, I reopened Norman's trunk and stared at the pile of books. One by one I removed them, more carefully this time. And there it was, dismissed the first time, either by haste or indifference, a small Bible, worn from over use. This was a gut-punch. Sitting on the cot, I opened it, and saw a web of underlined verses, not just on one page, but many pages. *I am the way, the truth and the light.* Another page. A circle around Jeremiah 29:11. *For I know the plans I have for you...plans to prosper you and not to harm you, plans to give you hope and a future.* Turning to the front I saw his handwritten inscription—*Norman Witt. Taken from a dead comrade's body at Saint-Germain-de-Varreville.*

I felt myself slumping. This Bible had been through the war with my father. It only took a closer examination to see the dotting of mud on some pages, and blood on some others, dried to a coppery brown. Was my father the reason for Reuben Flett's understanding of the Bible? Was this just one more thing denied me? I didn't know whether to rage or to cry. I was beginning to hate this place for the Pandora's Box it had become. How many more truths did I need?

I set the Bible on the pillow, and checking to make sure Nancy McGrath's station wagon was still gone, I crossed the lawn to the pump house. I stared at the padlock and the hasp that held it together on the door frame. The hasp itself looked ancient, lined with permanent rust, the padlock not much better. But what did I know about such things? What I did know, or thought I knew, was some strange energy was beckoning me; a force I could not explain, beseeching me to enter. It was like a howling in my ears.

For the first time I noticed I was sweating. The hot morning was getting hotter and it had become muggy. Turning again I looked at the approaching black clouds. They were taking their time, hovering ominously above the distant rim rock shelves, filling the full breadth of the open sky. For a moment I thought about my father's ashes, resting in a box, unattended inside a rock crevice of a cliff, a pile of rocks as a monument. And then I thought of Mercedes and my desire to get away from her. Had Mercedes been Ashley, I may never have come, because there would have been a contentment to a relationship like that. But it was Mercedes, a mismatch from the beginning, and so that discomfort set me on a railroad trip for what seemed a means of escape.

You're not here by accident, Sam. Oline's words.

At the very thought of her, I saw her in my mind. Full brown hair, handsome forehead, Grace Kelly eyebrows, and pretty lips. Up to that time I had only seen her as a waitress in a cafe in a lonely, strange, tumbleweed town. But now, the thought of Oline, in contrast to Nancy McGrath, pushed a deeper element of shame into me. I had thought I'd used my need for truth as a reason for succumbing to Nancy McGrath, but now it was plain to see that I had been the victim of her clever devices. It was she who had caught me in her web.

In disgust, I turned back down the hill. It was time to free myself of some well-deserved guilt.

There is a degree of embarrassment, sitting here in my study, and looking at all the shelves of books, trophies, keepsakes and mementos, that give it a museum atmosphere, where I, as curator, could point and talk about each item and launch into a full-blown explanation. My wife and I once visited a Hemingway museum in Arkansas where the big man lived for a while with his second wife, Pauline, at her parent's home. The barn had been converted into a work space where the still young writer pounded out one of his novels. I still recall the tour guide trying, and partially failing, to give a full panoramic of Hemingway's time there. It proved to me that at some point it is clear—you can't bring the full scope of a man's life to fit inside the space of a room full of photos and paraphernalia.

It is the pistol I am remembering now. The army issue Colt 45 that I found in Nancy McGrath's kitchen drawer that dark morning when I made my escape from her bedroom. It would eventually become clear that the pistol belonged to my father, a weapon he was able to bring home from the war; a pistol he had used to kill Nazi's. It is a pistol that bears its own story.

No farmer in Eltopia or the surrounding area wanted rain, not with wheat harvest only a month away, and all eyes seemed to be nervously studying the blackening sky with dread. The cafe was nearly full to capacity because I would learn later, farmers are a species that huddle together at such times. I heard from Reuben once how if a farmer was stricken with an illness, the neighbors were there to see his crop got harvested when he couldn't. Or if there was a wheat fire, fellow farmers left their own field to help put out the fire. Of course, Reuben turned it into a parable, about loving your neighbor.

And Reuben was among the company sitting in the cafe, alone at a booth eating a bowl of corn chowder. I slid in opposite him uninvited.

"You want a beer?"

I shook my head.

"You might as well. I'm having one. Might give you fortitude for tonight."

I looked around to see if anybody was listening.

"Don't worry. Oline already knows you're up to something."

I looked at him. "How?"

"Because you're still here. Train came through and left. And here you sit." He nodded towards the kitchen, and following his gaze I saw Oline staring at me, looking not perturbed, but askance, her blue eyes lasers. *How could I have missed this?* I wondered. I smiled back and suddenly realized that was probably the first time I had smiled since coming to Eltopia. It stretched my face uncomfortably, knowing I hadn't smiled much in my entire life.

My mind was doing paces now, skipping back and forth from a rusty padlock, the oncoming storm, Reuben's prodding tease, and Oline's blue eyes. Lost in all of that was Nancy McGrath, until, through the cafe window I saw her station wagon make its turn from the highway onto the gravel road. It left a cloud of dust from the dirt road leading to the post office.

When I turned back, Oline had scooted into the booth beside Reuben. Her expression was stern, and for a moment I felt like one of my own students who had just gotten one of my cross stares. I gave her a quizzical look.

"You both look guilty as sin," Oline said. "What are you up to?"

Reuben and I exchanged a glance.

Looking back, as I am doing here from my study, rain still pelting the window, my Cincinnati neighborhood a blur through the haze, I am convinced it was a pivotal moment in finding a deeper truth in who my father was, and to a greater extent, who *I* was. And who I would become. The glance that Reuben and I exchanged put a twist on the hours that would follow, and making a conspiracy of two become that of three. The words he had spoken to me, in reprimand that same morning, that I was not the only orphan in Eltopia, changed forever the landscape of our plans. It came down to trust. Sitting there, as the cafe emptied out, and with a nod from Reuben, we told Oline everything. Everything. Nothing was left out. Oline, to her credit, listened wordlessly, not a single interruption, though she did not conceal her shock at knowing that Norman Witt was not buried in that weed-infested cemetery on the hill, rather in a beloved crevice in the rim rocks.

Obviously there was no mention of my night in Nancy McGrath's bed, or of our planned attempt to break into the pump house. We had no desire to include her into what could be a criminal act. But our suspicions about Nancy McGrath's involvement in my father's death we did share, which was received with a solemn nod of her head. Reuben and I took that as a sign of agreement.

Reuben went back to the grain elevators and Oline returned to her work. For me it was a long afternoon and evening of waiting. Returning to the cabin, I took up his war Bible again, and began reading the New Testament, beginning with the book of Matthew. It was like reading *Gulliver's Travels*, so alive with detail and intrigue, that by nightfall I was well into the book of Luke. All through it came the distant sound of thunder. The storm had arrived, and it came just as Jesus walked on water through a storm, and how Peter ventured out of the boat. Was this undertaking at midnight a version of that, where faith in the unknown similar to that, taking a blind step into finding an end to my inner storm?

Closing my eyes, I slept for an hour, and was awakened by a quiet tapping on the door. Not Nancy McGrath, I hoped. But checking my watch I saw it was nearly midnight, and I opened the door and let Reuben in. The reading lamp was still on, and in the soft glow Reuben looked every bit like a noble Indian, one who just as well might have been painted up for war. He stood only long enough, with the door open, for me to see the rain, falling at a pitiful rate.

"We're going to get soaked," he said. "I'm already soaked."

I nodded, then put on my ball cap. For a long moment we stared at each other. Finally he turned and stepped out into the storm and I followed. The yard was dark, but halfway to the pump house a lightning bolt flashed overhead, lighting everything up as if it were daylight. Then darkness again. At the door, Reuben produced a small flashlight and he handed it to me to hold while he investigated the padlock and hasp. Producing a stiff wire from his pocket, he inserted it into the padlock, and after several turns and wiggles, the lock opened like magic. My heart rose to my throat.

Rain was dripping off the bill of my cap, my drenched shirt sticking to my back. I watched, nearly paralyzed with anticipation, as Reuben lifted the lock and opened the door. The rain had bloated the doorjamb so the door let out a pitiful groan as it opened. We stepped inside and with the flashlight, we poured over the interior. It was as Shim Harden had described, a slightly cluttered box of a room, the pump and its tank taking up the better part of the area.

The light beam, as if a trail of light doing its own snooping, searched out every corner, crack and crevice in the room. There was a musty odor, of old paper and mildew. Whatever Nancy McGrath may have done with the letters addressed to me that Shim saw, or the bag which I saw her bring in, were nowhere in sight. We checked the ceiling and the floor for a trap door of any kind, but there was none. Finally the beam turned on our faces and on our shared expressions of puzzlement and disappointment.

Reluctantly, I shrugged, and stepped to the door, when I felt Reuben's hand on my shoulder. Turning I saw him pointing to a loose board on the wall. We looked at it together. There was something out of place about it. It hung slightly cockeyed where the other boards were straight, and there was a nail partially protruding from it. Reuben reached up and pulled gently on the nail and the whole board fell away.

Suddenly I heard a voice, shrieking like a strangled cat. It was Nancy McGrath, and as I turned, standing in the doorway, I saw her dark form standing in the middle of the lawn.

"Get out," she screamed. Then, immediately, a flash of lightning illuminated her, standing in the rain, one arm extended, and in her hand was the Colt .45. Then darkness again. But next I saw the flash of the muzzle and the splintering thud of a bullet tearing into the old wood next to my head. Instinctively I dropped to my knees, just as another shot tore at the door frame. I could feel Reuben moving behind me, shielded by the wall.

Another flash of lightning, and this time what I saw was a madman in a woman's body, standing with legs apart and planted, her nightgown a sopping second skin clinging to her. "Get out," she screamed again, an utter wildness that would haunt my dreams ever after.

Then suddenly, a different voice, from out of the darkness by the cabin.

"Sam!"

In that instant, Nancy McGrath turned, and in a movement so fast I nearly missed it, Reuben Flett leaped over the top of me and sprinting straight on, collided with Nancy McGrath, knocking her to the ground. Another lightning flash showed the struggle and they wrestled for control of the pistol. Then darkness. Getting my bearings, I stumbled out of the door and ran to where they were rolling on the lawn. But by the time I got there, I saw that Reuben had the Colt in his hand, and Nancy McGrath was trying to get to her feet.

"Sam!" It was Oline's voice again.

"Stay back," I hollered.

The next flash showed Nancy McGrath running back to her house, the downpour like a curtain to a final act. But it wasn't the final act yet.

Reuben stood, holding the pistol. "Take care of her," he said, pointing to where Oline stood, soaked like the rest of us. Reaching her I steered her into the cabin and closed the door. We stood like soaked mongrels, both of us breathing heavily. Finally I managed, "What are you doing here?"

She gave no answer, so I held her to me, stupidly, as if my wetness would dry her out. Releasing her I saw the blanket on the cot and grabbed it, then wrapped it around her. "Stay here," I commanded.

Her voice stopped me at the door. "Sam Witt. Don't you tell me what to do."

I looked at her, and everything beautiful seemed to flood out of her at that moment. Her lovely hair was a dripping waterfall. Her makeup of the day were lined streaks running down her cheeks. Her lips shivering. It was a moment out of time. With scarce an ounce of reasoning, I took her face in my hands and kissed her. And then, like a coward, I fled.

What I was fleeing to was the opening chapter to the rest of my life.

Reuben had torn the loose board further, and was pulling off others, and with each removed board fell a cascade of envelopes, landing at his feet. I stared in disbelief. Behind me I could feel Oline's hand on my shoulder. Reaching down I picked up several of the envelopes and looked at them. Every one of them was addressed to me, Sammy Witt, at the tenement address in Cincinnati. Reuben stopped tearing at the boards. There were more letters hidden in the walls, but there was no more room at our feet.

It was the closest thing to a church service I had ever attended. I was on my knees, weeping shamelessly. I lifted the letters to me, holding them as if some beloved sacraments. For me, they were. Holy. Granted me twenty-six years too late. And the rain came down. And the lightning flashed and the thunder cracked.

Suddenly I could feel Oline stiffen. She had turned at the last flash of lightning and gasped. Looking up I saw Reuben's eyes wide as saucers. Clambering to my feet I waited for the next flash, and when it came, I saw the source of their horror. Through the bedroom window, I saw Nancy McGrath for the last time, hanging by her neck from the hook in the ceiling, her naked body turning slowly round.

It is with delicate care that I return to these memories. I am on my way soon to attend the memorial for my dead friend. To even imagine Reuben Flett no longer a living member of my inner circle is a hard pill to swallow. That night, in the storm, he did what countless Indians before him had done. He charged headlong, straight into the face of the enemy, and into possible death, and saved my life. For it was me that Nancy McGrath was trying to kill. The image of him, standing in the rain, surrounded by a lightning flash, and the loud roaring of thunder, pistol in hand, is no less a picture of Sitting Bull or Gall. Of Crazy Horse and Red Cloud. Of every warrior that stood in the face of extinction who held their ground.

It would be Reuben himself who would later show me how to

teach the history of the American people, white and black, red, yellow or brown, no matter the color. It was to recognize that the best of them could also be the worst of them, depending on the day and the circumstances. I know at this moment, I would give a year of my life, right now, to have seen Reuben one more time alive.

What followed was a week of investigations by the Franklin Country Sheriff's office. Nancy McGrath's suicide was undisputed, and even her reasoning behind it once the discovery of the wall full of my letters was shared with the authorities. But there was a further glimpse into the woman's madness when the house where she lived was gone through with a fine toothed comb. As I, myself, had gone through the dusty, unused rooms of her house, in the room that had no furniture but only the cot at the far wall, a corpse was discovered. By the time of the search, the corpse lying there under a thin blanket was close to utter petrification. A belated autopsy proved it to be that of her father. And that the cause of death estimated to be that of starvation. Nancy McGrath's father had not taken a job in Colorado, he had been murdered by his own daughter.

I spent many more days in the shower trying to purge myself from the evil sin of that woman, who like a fool I had soiled my soul with. But it was my letters, once freed to me by the authorities, nearly three hundred of them, which took every ounce of my courage to face. I had hated a man who loved me. There was no way to sugar coat or justify my misguided actions as a selfish, and self-pitying, toad of a human being. It took Reuben's wisdom to stir me into my own redemption. Sitting side by side on the cot in the cabin, going through the letters, he pointed again to Norman's war Bible.

"The world calls us fools for believing such fantasy," he said. "But fantasy it is not. Let the world go to Hell, Sam. But if you truly ever want to see your father again, believe every word of that book and you will. Because your father is where that book says he'll be. And already is."

Along with my father's letters, there was money. Usually a few one dollar bills, or some fives. On a couple of occasions, there would be a twenty. When it was all tallied up, it was into the thousands. If there is any credit given to Nancy McGrath, it is that it appeared she never opened a single letter. The untouched money seemed to indicate that.

Sammy, it is my regret that I left you so soon after coming home. I never realized how unfair that was to both of us. I never was able to tell you about how, in the freezing nights on the Bulge, it was you on my mind as much as the Germans.

Hence, my education began. Reuben's old pickup held up, journey after journey, as he taught me to see the rugged beauty of the flat, sagebrush filled land where his people once chased horses through the basalt ravines, across the Blue Mountains, following the Columbia River and the Snake River to where they merged into history. It made me forget about any text book I had ever used. With notebook and pen; with simple Kodak camera; I sat under the tutelage of Reuben Flett, and in a more mystical degree, to my father, who had once walked this prairie, and touched the rich earth with his hands.

...our passion is made up of things almost unknowable to us, Sam. I can't explain it properly. But the war, and the things I saw in that war, have reshaped me. I have been put on the pottery wheel, son, and slowly been reshaped into something highly more meaningful than anything I ever was before.

Norman Witt's letters to his only son were works of art. So great were they to me that they put a small scale to the Grand Coulee Dam, so massive in it girth and architecture. The letters, all boxed now, both the war letters and those secreted in the pump house wall, are sitting right there in the corner of my overcrowded study. Reading them is not for the faint of heart. They are cruel in their breathtaking honesty, of both love and disappointment. Through his words I learned that yes, indeed, he had come back to Cincinnati, three times, expressively to see me and my sister and move the family out west to be with him. But it was my mother's bitterness, and eventual self-hatred, that barred the door. The last time, when I was about ten, she called the police on him, and he ended up spending a night in jail for supposedly harassing the woman he was still married to.

...and there I stood, Sammy, like a coward, looking down on your sleeping face. I touched your hair, letting my fingers feel your warmth. You didn't

I stayed in Eltopia too long, and not long enough. But I was a teacher, and it was approaching the third week in July. Reuben was in full swing of wheat harvest and the trucks filled with grain were lined up all day long in front of the warehouse to dump their loads. Oline too was in the cafe's high season, with farmers and field hands clambering in for soup and sandwiches. I was lucky to get a glance as I sat in a corner booth with my father's war Bible.

One day, as I was packing things up and putting things in order for the long train ride home, I heard a light knock on the cabin door.

"Can I come in?" It was Oline.

Inside she sat on the cot and watched me put the last of my things in my suitcase. Nancy McGrath's house was boarded up, but the sheriff's department granted me permission to use the cabin to full extent, which I had. I had put all of my father's letters in the war chest and locked it back up. It was too much to take on the train, so Reuben promised to put a padlock on the cabin, and I, in return, promised to come back for them, maybe by the next summer. It would be three summers before I came, in a Pontiac, which I filled the backseat full of Norman Witt's world.

"When are you leaving?"

I looked at Oline. Her face was turned slightly away from me, and a sunbeam, which had penetrated the window, had fallen across half her face, and staring at her I realized my mouth had come open slightly. I blinked, mindlessly unaware of her heart, only of her face.

"This afternoon," I said.

She nodded.

"I'm not working today. Can I walk down to the train with you?"

A little of the old Sam was at battle inside me. I remembered the kiss I had given her, in this very room. It seemed a life time ago. For Nancy McGrath, it was a lifetime ago. I sat down beside Oline and put my hand on hers.

"Parting is such sweet sorrow. Who said that?"

Without looking at me, she said, "Juliet. Spoken to Romeo. *That I shall say good night till it be morrow.*

We met the train together, standing in the gravel road, each of us watching to the south for the first sign of the engine, and the snake trailing behind. I had a head full of words but spoke none of them. Inside, I felt like that loner boy of the tenements again, fighting my way to survival; that hollow shell of loneliness that I somehow felt I deserved. Before I climbed onto the train, I faced her, and felt, strangely, that I was facing a mirror of myself. I hugged her feebly, knowing she wanted more, and as the train pulled away, I saw her standing alone, head up, brown and beautiful hair aflutter in the train's airy wake.

I won't live forever. Retiring from teaching at the end of next year will not guarantee a long life, but one makes his best efforts. And leaving teaching will be like a death in itself, as it has been something as close to me as the very blood that traffics my veins. I will miss it. Just a week ago, right before school was out and just before I got this disturbing telegram, Henry Ottoman stopped by my classroom. He looks younger than the man I first met thirty years ago, young in terms of vitality. He walks every day, but never alone. It is the PE teacher, long without love herself that walks with him, matching each other's strides. But it is not the walking, or the better diet that gives him such vibrancy. It is new love. Love lost and love re-found.

...snow falls, falling on our backs until we are nothing more than snowmen, and the trees, which were torn apart in the last war, might wonder what God has against them. And we might ask the same thing, but God owes us nothing, all the while giving us everything. If there is fear in you, Sammy, or simple wondering, always take the brave way...

The train stopped in Ritzville again and I stepped down, stretching my legs, pacing the platform, and feeling like the last time I was here was a hundred years ago. I avoided the ticket master and his cantankerous remarks, true as they turned out to be. If I was a smoker, this would be the perfect time to light up a cigarette and put on the casual pose, but I did not smoke. And there was nothing casual about the torment in my mind.

A summer dragonfly began doing a dance above my head, and turning to watch it I caught a full-faced reflection of myself in the depot's amber window. I squinted, as if seeing a stranger, and suddenly I felt I was waking up, not from sleep, but from the dead. My whole life seemed to be staring back at me, and the pieces I was seeing of myself were not of comfort or reassurance, rather falseness and cowardliness. I could see the far distant face of Ashley, the affection I had for her had grown out of love and into respect. Mercedes was there too, in mocking pose, pretending to be happy, but the long ago collapse of her facade, revealing the sad woman she would always be.

Who are you? I asked the reflection. Have you ever in your life taken a chance? Even this trip to Eltopia was taken for all the wrong reasons. But by way of providence, as Reuben had said, I found my father after all. I found his words and I found his love. And now, through all that I had learned in that little town, I believed I would see him again someday. My eyes fell and I was ashamed, but then heard a voice in my head, saying the right words—*Do you think you got here by accident?*

It was closing time and I could see Oline through the window, her lovely brown hair, the way it touched her shoulders, and she stood, a trace of challenge in the way she expressed her confidence, and even in a greasy, coffee stained apron, she knew who she was and what she was about. I watched her take a final swipe at the counter with her washcloth. Then turning, she said something to the cook, who was just then turning out the kitchen lights.

From a peg she took up a light sweater to wear on her walk to her uncle's house through the chilly prairie night. Without looking back, she waved one last time to the cook, and opened the front door into the growing summer darkness. Two steps off the porch and she saw me. Even the way she paused, standing briefly on one leg, then shifting to the other, I felt myself turn lighter than air. There was nothing in the world I wanted at that moment more than to look into those blue eyes and know that my being here was the best thing I had ever done.

She came to me slowly, testing the space between us, and finally, tipping her head in a faint nod, said, "Sam Witt."

———————

Oline is standing in the doorway, looking at her wristwatch, a watch given her by somebody else, not me, and though she doesn't like wearing watches, she feels it might be a thing to have with her on the plane ride to Spokane. She gives me a familiar look. Our marriage has not been without struggles, raising the kids and meeting the challenges of our teaching careers. But nothing ever came between us that was not remedied by going back to that cabin, and that first rain-soaked kiss.

In my mind, even as we are about to call for the taxi, I can still see her traipsing the garden beds at Jefferson's Monticello, so absorbed in her own world that not even I was worth a look up at from her joy. Only the herbs, only the bean rows, only the raspberry hedges. It made me realize that you can love someone and still have to share them with that part of their heart that God specifically formed, before the beginning of time.

Dear Sam – I'm coming to see you. I'll be in Cincinnati in a couple of weeks. Expressly to see you. It's long overdue. Nothing but death will keep me from seeing you again, grown man that you are now. For too long I have held tight to a false memory. But son, know this—memory and truth are not always the same thing. In the end it is up to each of us to choose which to believe. No man can deny another man's truth. If you'll have me, you'll know mine.

Acknowledgments

The beginning of this project goes back more than twenty years. Once started, it was benched a number of times, and after each resurrection, it was benched again. But in the end, the story remained too close to my writer's heart to ignore. My fond thanks goes out to a small desk under a window in a Stockton, California, retail tire store, where newly inspired I put the finishing touches on *Eltopia* with kudos to my son, manager Matt Buchmann, who provided the inspiring setting.

As in all of my books, Jennifer Moorman deserves my deepest gratitude for being not only my chief editor but also my coach and constant encourager. We've been working partners through this, *Eltopia*, my eighteenth book. Likewise, Alexandria Mullins, my cover designer puts the final pizzazz to every finished project, giving each book its showcase appeal.

My assistant editor, Joslin Kier of Ephrata, Washington, does a great deal of the heavy lifting that goes into finding and correcting, not only my grammatical errors but also giving me styling input.

Many thanks to my son, Alex J. E. Buchmann for his help with character development.

Many thanks do I offer to Cynthia Dano of Moses Lake, my cover photographer who traveled the back roads and byways of this wide open farm country to capture the perfect interpretation for *Eltopia*.

Add to this the Giver of gifts, my Lord and Savior, Jesus.

About the Author

E. Hank Buchmann is a native son of Eastern Washington State, living and writing from his hometown, Moses Lake. He has traveled extensively throughout the United States and places in both Europe and Asia. But home is home, and *Eltopia* is his tribute to the glorious land of the Columbia River Big Bend country.

www.ingramcontent.com/pod-product-compliance
Lightning Source LLC
Chambersburg PA
CBHW020930160726
47993CB00005B/2212